From Feud to Forever

Willow Glen Book One

Juliet McKinley

Dedication

For the ones who've ever had to start over—
who've learned that forgiveness is messy, healing isn't linear,
and sometimes love circles back when you least expect it.
This one's for you.

From the Author

This story first appeared in the *Hates Mates* anthology, a special charity collection created in honor and memory of Catherine Wiltcher.

All proceeds from that anthology were donated to Bowel Cancer U.K., supporting vital research and raising awareness for a cause close to many hearts.

I'm honored to have been a part of it—and grateful to now share this story with you here.

Prologue

Christiane

The cold bites deeper in the French countryside than it ever did in the city. I pull my coat tighter around me as I step out of the farmhouse for the last time. Frost coats the overgrown path, crunching under my boots. The land is quiet—too quiet. There are no voices, no laughter echoing from the kitchen, no soft humming from *Maman* as she kneads dough. Just the wind and the grief that clings like fog.

Burying Papa Mark next to my mother and father was the final thread tying me to the life I once knew. I held his hand until the very end. Sorted through his paperwork in a home that had once been filled with warmth and was now stripped bare. I even found the old recipe book my mother used to read from when I couldn't sleep. The pages still smelled faintly of cinnamon.

It took weeks to prove his rights to the land and honor his wish to be laid to rest on it. But in the end, there wasn't enough left to hold onto. The debts strangled the farm slowly. Quietly. Like ivy around the bones of something once solid.

I used to think the land would always be there—quiet and steady, the way Papa Mark's hands were when he taught me to shape dough or fix a fence post. But even the strongest things can rot from the inside when no one's looking.

Selling it wasn't just a loss. It was an erasure.

I didn't just leave my home. I left ghosts behind. My *maman*'s scarf still hung by the back door. Her wedding dishes lined the cabinet, chipped but cherished. Papa Mark's boots were still by the fire. Empty.

The land is sold. The home is gone. I have thirty days to vacate. Thirty days to figure out where I'm going, what I'm doing—and if there's anything left of me to carry into whatever comes next.

That night, I collapse onto the hard mattress of a tiny hotel room in town, my coat still on, my fingers still shaking. I should sleep. Make a plan in the morning. Be logical. But my mind refuses to stop spinning. Every time I close my eyes, I see empty hallways and unlit rooms.

So instead, I scroll numbly through my phone—just noise, just motion—until an ad flickers across the screen.

Property Auction—Final 24 Hours

I click without thinking. Just something to do. I scroll through the listings: too far, too expensive, too broken. Then I stop.

A farmhouse.

Willow Glen, New York. Five acres. Two stories. A wraparound porch and enough charm peeking through the weathered siding to make my chest ache. The kind of house I might've imagined as a child if I'd believed in fairy tales. The price is low. Too low. No offers. It needs work—a lot—but it's livable.

I stare at the screen. I have the money. Barely. Is this stupid? Reckless? Is it selfish to want to put down roots again so soon?

My rational side says wait. Think. Make a plan.

But another part of me—smaller but louder—whispers something else.

What if this is the last chance to choose something for yourself?

The bid confirmation stares back at me.

My chest tightens with something sharp and irrational: fear or hope, maybe both. I tell myself it's just a house. Just land. But something inside me curls tight around the idea.

What if it's more?

Before I can talk myself out of it, I sign up, fill out the form, and place the bid.

Then I shut off my phone and wait.

Chapter One

Christiane

Two weeks later, I step off the plane into the bitter New York wind. It slices through me like a blade, whipping into my collar, stinging my ears, stealing my breath. I didn't expect to feel so untethered arriving here. But the moment my boots hit American soil, the weight of it all settles in my chest. The last time I was here, I had a family. A home. Now I have neither.

The auction went through. The farmhouse is mine.

I rent a truck and head to Willow Glen, GPS blinking quietly on the dash. The drive from the airport is long and winding, cutting through quiet stretches of snow-dusted trees and sleepy towns. With each passing mile, my nerves shift and tighten; hope and fear warring in my chest.

As I near the outskirts of Willow Glen, the landscape opens up. Rolling hills. Faded barns. The kind of place where time moves slower. I pass a general store, a diner with a peeling sign, and finally turn onto a gravel road flanked by bare trees and old stone fences. My heart hammers in my chest as the farmhouse comes into view.

It's the first time I'm seeing it with my own eyes. Worn wood, peeling paint, a porch that sags under decades of weather and waiting. But it's beautiful.

Not in the polished, catalog-perfect way. No, this kind of beauty is quiet. Earned. Waiting for someone to believe in it again.

I park the truck and get out slowly, the cold air biting at my cheeks. My boots crunch over gravel and patchy grass as I take in the view one more time—my new home, raw and waiting. But before I can let myself sink into it, I check the time and climb back into the truck.

I've got one more stop to make.

The goat farm I found online is just a few miles outside of town. It takes longer than expected to find the turnoff, and even longer to bounce down the rutted dirt drive. But when I pull up beside a barn with a slanted roof and weathered fence posts, a man steps out to meet me, wiping his hands on a rag.

"You Christiane?"

I nod. "You've got goats for sale?"

"Sure do. Come take a look."

He leads me toward a pen where three brown-and-white goats sniff curiously at my outstretched hand. They're sturdy, well-trained, and perfect for milking. The farmer leans against the fence, arms crossed, his flannel stained with feed dust and patience.

"She's the best of the bunch," he says, nodding toward one of the does as she tugs playfully at my coat. "Easy to handle. Feed her right, and she'll give you more milk than you know what to do with."

I smile—really smile—for the first time in weeks. It feels strange. Like something stretching after being asleep too long. But this moment? This feels real. The cold air, the hay underfoot, the sound of braying from the barn. This is something I can build on.

"You got any cows?" I ask suddenly.

The man raises a brow. "Just one. Jersey mix, solid temperament. Sweet girl."

He leads me around the side of the barn where a docile milk cow stands under a lean-to, lazily chewing hay. She's smaller than Papa Mark's Cookie, but something about her big brown eyes and gentle face makes my chest ache.

"She got a name?"

"Not really. Never stuck with one."

I reach out and stroke her neck. She leans into the touch, and I close my eyes for a second, letting the moment settle.

"I'll take her too," I say softly.

The farmer gives a low chuckle. "You starting a petting zoo or a farm?"

"A new life," I answer. "Hopefully."

We settle the details as the sun dips low behind the barn. I sign the paperwork with hands still chilled from the drive, arrange for hay delivery, and load the goats into the truck with more care than experience. The cow takes a little more coaxing, but she goes without fuss, her soft eyes blinking slow and sweet as if she already understands she's coming home with me. I name her Cookie. It's not the same cow, of course. But the name feels like a bridge—something I can carry forward from the past without pretending nothing has changed.

Just as I'm about to thank him and head back to the truck, a flicker of movement catches my eye. Off to the side, tucked behind the main pens, a smaller enclosure holds a single black goat.

He stares at me like he's already over the conversation—small and scrappy, eyes glittering with mischief. As I watch, he noses at the latch on the gate, gives it a deliberate nudge, then glances over his shoulder like he's gauging whether anyone's watching.

"What about him?" I ask, nodding toward the pen.

The farmer lets out a weary laugh. "That one? Trouble with a capital T. Smart as hell. Climbs fences, opens gates, once let the whole herd out and tried to lead them into my kitchen. Name's Emmanuel—after my brother-in-law. Same flair for chaos."

I can't help the startled laugh that escapes me. "Seriously?"

"Dead serious. He's a gremlin. Got a mind of his own and a nose for mischief."

My laughter softens into something more thoughtful. "What happens to him?"

The farmer's expression dims. "Can't keep him. Can't sell him. Someone's coming tomorrow for slaughter."

"Slaughter? Just because he's clever?"

He shrugs. "Clever doesn't pay the feed bill. You want him, he's yours—but don't say I didn't warn you."

I don't even pause. "I'll take him."

The farmer blinks. "You sure?"

I nod. "Yeah. I think I could use a little chaos."

He mutters something under his breath but unlatches the pen. I crouch down and hold out my hand.

Emmanuel approaches slowly, sniffs, and promptly head-butts the gate like it's a test of wills.

I huff a quiet laugh. "Yeah," I murmur. "You'll fit right in."

The gravel spits under my tires as I roll to a stop, dust curling in the mirrors like smoke. For a moment, I can't make myself move. The farmhouse waits ahead, hunched against the sky, a little too quiet, a little too still. Not the dream I carried across the ocean, but the reality I bought with shaking hands and a stubborn heart.

I shut off the engine, and silence crashes in. No farm dogs barking. No kettle clanging from a kitchen window. No *Maman's* voice calling me inside. Only the thin whine of wind weaving through pine and the long creak of porch boards as if the house itself is shifting in its sleep.

The sight should scare me. The porch sagging, shutters hanging loose, the windows dull and clouded. But what I feel most is a pulse of determination, sharp and insistent. This place is mine. Cracked or not, broken or not. I came here to build something, and I will.

I open the door and step out, rocks crunching beneath my boots. The air is sharp with the scent of pine and damp earth. The barn looms a few yards away, its red paint sun-faded and curling, but the bones still steady. Emmanuel bleats from the trailer, already plotting his first escape. Cookie shifts beside him, calm and solemn as always. My heart aches just looking at her; my one piece of stability in this chaos.

As I round the house imagining where a garden might go, the deep rumble of an approaching engine cuts through my thoughts. A moving truck pulls into the drive, tires spitting gravel. Relief loosens the knot in my chest. Everything I could salvage from France is inside that truck—furniture, equipment, boxes stuffed with memories. What survived. What I couldn't leave behind.

I wave to the driver as he hops down, but before I can greet him, a sharp movement snatches my attention. A man storms toward me from the neighboring property, long strides eating up the distance, his face dark with anger. Broad shoulders, weathered lines, graying hair clipped close. His presence is a storm all its own.

"Hey!" His voice cracks like a whip, sharp enough to startle the goats in the trailer. "What the hell do you think you're doing?"

My breath hitches. I square my shoulders, meeting his glare head-on. "Excuse me?"

"This property isn't yours," he growls, stopping just feet away. "I don't know who you are, but you can't just squat in an empty house and claim it."

His assumptions cut deep. That I don't belong. That I'm stealing. That I'm nothing more than a trespasser.

"I'm not squatting," I say evenly. "I bought this property."

He scoffs, eyes narrowing. "That's impossible. I'm buying this property."

I cross my arms. "Well that's news to me. Because, according to the deed and the appraisal district records, this land belongs to me."

"You're lying."

My hands tremble as I pull out my phone. "I'm not. And if you don't believe me, we can call the authorities and sort this out."

His nostrils flare. "You don't need to call anyone."

"Oh, I think I do." My thumb slick with sweat, I pull up the proof of sale and tax records, holding the screen out. "Here. Read it for yourself. Christiane. That's me." I point to myself just in case he needs more clarification.

He doesn't reach for the phone. Just stares. A muscle ticks in his cheek, jaw working.

After a long pause, he exhales sharply and steps back. "Damn it," he mutters. "I was supposed to buy this place."

"Well you didn't." My voice shakes, but I don't look away. "I did."

He drags a hand through his hair, resentment flickering in his eyes. "This isn't over," he says, then turns on his heel and stalks back across the field.

I watch him go, heart still pounding. Some welcome wagon. The hope I carried here feels like it's leaking out through the soles of my boots.

A loud thump from the trailer jerks my attention. Then another. Followed by a bleat.

I whirl just in time to see Emmanuel vault off the ramp like a tiny goat-shaped rocket, hooves clicking wildly as he prances into the yard. He charges the overgrown flowerbed, nibbles a dormant rosebush, then headbutts the side of the porch.

"Emmanuel!" I lunge forward. "*Comment as-tu fait ça? How did you get out?*"

He bleats in reply—the picture of innocence—and trots a few feet ahead, tail flicking like he's the one giving the tour.

I press a hand to my temple, laughing despite myself. For the first time in months, the sound feels real.

"You little troublemaker. You're going right into the barn."

He ignores me, of course, launching onto a pile of wood with an arrogant bleat.

I sigh and glance back at the house, the barn, and the land I now call mine. The foundation might be cracked. The paint might be peeling. The neighbors might be feral.

But it's mine.

For so long, only silence has filled me. But here, on this land, something whispers louder.

Hope.

Chapter Two

Adam

I slam the barn door shut behind me harder than I mean to, the wood rattling against its frame. Dust shakes loose from the rafters, drifting down through the beams of late afternoon sun like ash after a fire. My chest is heaving, breath sharp, pulse still kicking up a storm after that encounter with the Frenchwoman next door.

Bought it. She said she bought the farm.

I've been working with the bank, waiting for paperwork, fighting tooth and nail to reclaim what was stolen from my family. That land was supposed to be mine. *My land!* And now, out of nowhere, some stranger shows up, talking about deeds and appraisals like she knows what any of it means.

My boots echo across the barn floor as I pace, the air thick with hay and manure and the faint tang of motor oil. The goats bleat from their pen, restless from all the shouting. Even the old horse shifts uneasily, stamping against the boards. I rake a hand over my face, trying to shove down the fury rising inside me.

Because the truth is, I saw the phone screen she shoved in my face. The deed had her damn name on it.

I kick at a loose piece of straw, the sound too small for the rage filling me. "Damn it," I mutter, fists clenching at my sides.

That farm was supposed to be my way of putting things right. My way of undoing at least a fraction of the damage Papa caused. He gambled away half our land, drank through the rest, and left me with nothing but debt and dirt under my nails. I've spent twenty years clawing back every acre I could, and now? Now some woman who doesn't even belong here is planting herself in the middle of it like she owns the damn valley.

Because, apparently, she does.

I stalk toward the workbench, the one place that usually calms me. Tools hang in neat rows above it—hammers, wrenches, saws—all sharpened, polished, oiled. A farmer's arsenal. My arsenal. I should pick something up, lose myself in a task, and channel my anger into fixing it instead of breaking.

But before I can, a sharp thud rattles the wall.

I freeze, frown, then glance at the door. Another thud follows, lighter this time, as if something or someone had pressed against the wood.

I stride back and yank the door open.

And there she is.

The Frenchwoman. Christiane, she'd said her name was. Standing in the doorway with her arms full of goat, of all things. The little black menace squirms against her, bleating like it's in on some private joke. She looks at me with wide, startled eyes, strands of hair sticking to her flushed cheeks, and for a moment, the fight drains right out of me.

"What the hell are you doing on my land?" I demand, gruffer than I mean to.

Before she can answer, the goat wriggles free with a triumphant bleat and bolts between my legs, darting deeper into the barn like he's been living here all along.

"Emmanuel, *espèce de petit démon*!" she snaps, throwing her hands in the air. "*Viens ici tout de suite!*"

I don't know what she just said, but I'm pretty damn sure it wasn't a compliment.

She rushes past me without so much as a second glance, boots clattering across the concrete floor as she chases after the black blur weaving between hay bales. I should stop her. Should tell her to get off my property and take her damn troublemaker with her.

But instead, I lean against the doorframe, watching the chaos unfold.

"Get back here, you goat!" she hisses, half English, half French, ducking after him as he leaps onto a pile of hay like it's his throne. "*Merde zut alors tu es un cauchemar!*"

I only catch one word in that string, but the look she throws me when she realizes I'm still standing there makes me bite back a laugh. She's breathless, cheeks pink, hair tumbling loose from its braid, and she looks equal parts furious and embarrassed.

"You mind explaining why your goat thinks my barn is his playground?" I ask.

She glares, swiping at a loose strand of hair. "Because he is stubborn and stupid and," she growls another string of French I don't bother trying to untangle, "because the gate latch broke. He ran. I ran after him. And now…" She throws her hands up. "Now here we are."

Her goat chooses that moment to bleat again, smug as sin. I cross my arms, shaking my head. "Figures. Even your livestock's got no respect for property lines."

Her eyes flash, sharp as glass. "Maybe your barn shouldn't look so welcoming."

She's quick, nimble, weaving through the hay bales with surprising ease, her boots kicking up dust as she lunges for the goat. Emmanuel leaps onto a stack of crates, tail flicking, bleating triumphantly like he knows he's winning. And the sound that bursts out of her?

Laughter.

Light, sharp, unexpected. It echoes through the barn rafters and slides under my skin in a way I don't like.

I grit my teeth. "Does he do this often?"

She huffs, straightening when the goat finally settles on a bale, chewing smugly on some hay. She tucks a strand of hair behind her ear, cheeks still pink from the chase. "His name is Emmanuel. He likes to make trouble."

"No kidding," I mutter.

She squares her shoulders again, turning that sharp gaze on me. "Look, I don't want a fight. I bought this land fair and square, and whether you like it or not, I'm your neighbor now. If you've got a problem with that, take it up with the bank, not me."

The words hit harder than I want them to. Because she's right. Hell, I know she's right. But it doesn't stop the fire in my chest from burning hotter.

"I watched that listing for months," I snap, the bitterness scraping raw in my throat. "That land should've been mine. My family's. I had plans for it."

Her expression shifts and softens in a way I don't expect. Just a flicker, a crack in her armor. Grief pools in her eyes, so quick I almost miss it, swallowed by something heavier. "I'm sorry," she says quietly, her voice tight. "But it isn't yours. It's mine now. And I don't plan on leaving."

For a long moment, we just stand there. The barn quiets, even Emmanuel going still, chewing lazily as if he's satisfied with the chaos he caused. Dust drifts in the golden light, and all I can hear is the pounding of my own heart.

I want to hate her. Need to. It'd be easier that way.

But instead, I'm stuck noticing the way her accent curls around the words, the way her hands tremble slightly from nerves, the way she doesn't back down even though I'm twice her size and twice as furious.

Damn stubborn woman.

Finally, I drag a hand through my hair and step back, giving her space. "This isn't over," I mutter, because it's all I've got left.

Her mouth tightens, but she doesn't argue. Just turns toward the goat again, coaxing him down from the bale with a patience I don't have.

I watch her lead him out of the barn, sunlight catching on the edges of her hair, and the strangest thought strikes me: maybe the land isn't the only thing slipping out of my hands.

Chapter Three
Christiane

The morning air bites at my bare feet as I pad into the kitchen, the hush of dawn wrapping itself around me like a shawl. The boards creak under my weight, and the chill seeps up through the soles of my feet, sharp enough to make me shiver. I light the old stove and let it warm while I set out the items I bought on the drive here yesterday—flour, butter, coffee, sugar, and salt. Not much, but enough. A lifeline in brown paper bags.

I roll up my sleeves, dust the counter, and pour the flour in a mound. The butter is cold and stubborn under my hands, but soon it softens, blending with the flour until the dough yields. My fingers know these movements without thought. *Maman's* voice floats through memory, firm but gentle: *"Pas trop. Soft hands make soft biscuits."*

The scent of baking fills the kitchen, rich and steady, and for a moment I almost believe I am back in France on a Sunday morning with sunlight spilling across tiled floors. I close my eyes and press my palms flat against the counter, willing the ache in my chest to ease. It doesn't.

When the biscuits are golden, I break one open, steam curling into the air. A pat of butter melts instantly, pooling in the flaky layers. I take a bite and nearly laugh at the sound I make—hunger and longing tangled together. I brew coffee, intense and dark, and carry both outside to the porch.

The swing groans when I settle into it, but it holds. From here, I can see the land stretch out soft and wide, fog hugging the fence posts, dew turning the grass silver. And beyond the field—across the worn barbed-wire fence—is another farmhouse. His.

Even from this distance, I can see the shape of Adam's barn, the pale wash of the roofline, the faint curl of smoke from the chimney. Too close for comfort. If I step into the yard, I feel like I'm on a stage with him always watching from the wings.

I sip my coffee and pull my knees to my chest. *This is mine,* I remind myself. Even if he hates it.

By midmorning, I've unpacked the essentials. Dishes in the cupboards. Clothes folded into drawers. My toothbrush is in the bathroom, my photo of *Maman* and Papa Mark is propped on the mantel. They watch me as I move, their faces captured in one of the few pictures I managed to save. *Maman's* curls, her wide smile. Papa Mark beside her, steady and warm. My throat tightens.

"They'd be proud of me," I whisper. The words feel fragile. "I hope."

I press my fingertips to the glass, then force myself to move. There's work to do. The goats and Cookie will need more feed soon, which means today I have to venture into Willow Glen properly.

The truck rattles as I guide it into town, the gravel spitting under the tires before it gives way to pavement. Willow Glen rises like a storybook—quaint storefronts with painted signs, flower boxes spilling petunias, a clock tower chiming above Main Street. It feels... untouched. Like time runs slower here.

I pull up in front of the feed store, nerves humming as I climb out. The bell above the door jingles when I push it open, releasing the smell of hay, leather, and grain. It smells like every farm supply shop I've ever known, and yet it feels foreign because I'm the stranger here.

The man behind the counter, Jake according to his nametag, looks up from a ledger and grins. "Morning, miss. What can I do for ya?"

"I need supplies for my goats and Cookie, my milk cow," I say, smoothing my accent, trying not to feel self-conscious. "Feed, bedding, hay delivery if you can. And some chicks, if you have them."

He nods, jotting it down. "Got a batch of chicks in yesterday. Planning to start an egg business?"

"Just for me, for now. Maybe more later." I smile, faint but discernible. "Starting small."

The door swings open behind me, and cold air rushes at my ankles. Then comes a voice I recognize, sharp enough to cut.

"Here to buy up the rest of the town too?"

I turn slowly. Him. The man from yesterday, thundercloud face and arms folded like a wall.

"I'm just taking care of my animals," I say evenly, forcing my chin high.

Before he can snap back, another man steps forward, broad-shouldered with steady eyes. "I'm Patrick," he says, extending a hand. "This is Brandon. Eli's probably off stirring up trouble somewhere."

His handshake is firm, kind. "Nice to meet you," I manage, though my gaze keeps flicking to the scowling one behind him.

Brandon grins, easy and quick. "Damn, Adam, you always this charming?"

So that's his name. Adam. The sound of it coils in my chest, sharper than I expect.

Patrick clears his throat, redirecting. "So you're settling in all right?"

I hesitate, then nod. "It's a lot of work, but I'm getting there."

Adam doesn't say a word. Just watches me like he's waiting for me to trip. My fingers tremble as I pass Jake the cash for my order. I keep my smile pinned in place until I step outside.

The sidewalks are clean, the shop windows tidy. I walk slower, trying to breathe through the tightness in my chest. A bakery window fogs and I'm greeted with the scent of cinnamon. A florist arranges a wreath in the sun. For a moment, it almost feels like I could belong here.

Then I see it.

A neon sign above the glass reads *Maggie's Diner*. In the window, a weathered *For Sale* sign tilts against the glass.

Curious, I push the door open. The bell chimes, releasing warmth and the scent of coffee and sugar. A few customers linger in booths. Behind the counter, a woman looks up, her smile warm.

"Well, hello there," she says, wiping her hands on her apron. "Don't believe I've seen you before."

"Just moved in," I reply, offering a small smile. "Christiane."

"I'm Maggie. This here's my place—for now." Her glance flicks to the sign. "Been running it nearly thirty years. But my grandbabies are getting older, and I'd rather be chasing them than frying eggs."

I look around at the chipped tile floors, the sunlit counters, the pastry case half full. It feels worn but loved.

"You bake these?" I ask, nodding toward the pastries.

She beams. "Every morning before dawn. My mama taught me, same as hers."

A pang hits sharply. "My *maman* taught me too. We wanted to open a patisserie together, but she passed before we could."

Maggie's hand brushes mine. "It sounds like she raised you well."

"The best." My throat tightens.

An idea flickers. Small, fragile. "What if..." I hesitate, then shake my head.

"What if what?" Maggie prods, smiling.

"What if I made something new of this place? Not a patisserie, but... something that honors both of our families. A diner with bread that tastes like home."

Her brows rise, amused but thoughtful. "You serious?"

"Not yet," I admit. "But maybe one day."

She studies me for a long moment, then nods. "Dreams start small, honey. You just keep baking. We'll talk."

By the time I step back into the sunlight, the idea is rooted. Small but alive. Like a seed in good soil.

Across the street, a shadow leans against a truck. Arms crossed. Watching.

Adam.

My chest tightens, the fragile thread of hope tugs taut again.

I lift my chin, square my shoulders, and walk on.

Because this time, I'm not leaving.

Chapter Four
Adam

The Willow Glen farmers' market isn't where I get work done.

It's where people *play* at farming—polish their apples until they shine, stand behind stalls in clean boots, and charge triple for the same tomatoes you can pick up at the feed store.

But I come once a month. Keeps me in good graces with the old-timers, lets me trade an unwanted calf for fresh pork or hay for sweet corn without counting pennies, and—I'll admit it—I like walking through a place that smells like hay, fried dough, and wood smoke.

The gravel crunches under my boots as I cut through the crowd. Sun's already got bite to it, flashing off windshields and making me squint. The air's cold enough to keep breath visible, and someone's roasting cinnamon almonds three stalls over; the smell curls in the back of my throat. Kids dart between tables like barn cats, sticky with kettle corn, parents trailing behind with coffee cups clutched like lifelines.

Half the folks here I've known since I was old enough to wander down on my own with a couple of dollars and the promise I'd be back before dark. Mrs. Dobbins is selling her goat cheese, same as always, her silver hair sticking out from under a ball cap. She once kicked me clean out of her barn for chasing her granddaughter with a garter snake. I still can't look at her without thinking of the way she slammed that door behind me.

And then there *she* is.

Christiane.

Easy to spot. Her table's draped in a green check cloth, baskets lined in soldier-straight rows like they're waiting for a photograph. Loaves of bread, jars of jam, scones dusted with sugar so fine it catches the light. Even her damn *chalkboard signs* look like they belong in a magazine, curling handwriting spelling out things like *Blackberry-Vanilla Jam* and *Peach-Ginger Scones*.

She's laughing with some guy in a ball cap, handing him change like she's been here her whole life.

My boots slow down without my permission.

I could keep walking. Should keep walking. But my feet veer toward her stall.

When I stop in front of her table, she's mid-sentence with a woman pushing a stroller. Doesn't see me right away. I lean against the edge of her display and wait.

Her eyes flick up and that smile dies, replaced with a mask polite enough to make strangers feel welcome but pointed enough to keep me at arm's length.

"Didn't realize you were running a charity," I say.

She blinks. "Pardon?"

I nod toward her prices. "You're practically giving those away. Unless you plan on starving, I'd suggest charging what they're worth."

Her chin tilts. "Thank you for your unsolicited business advice, Mr. Williams. How's that working out for you?"

"It's working fine. I'm not bankrupt yet." I pick up a jar of jam, turn it in my hands. The glass is warm from sitting in the sun. "What's this supposed to be? Soup?"

Her eyes narrow. "That's *Blackberry-Vanilla Jam.* Hand-picked berries. And no, it's not runny. You might be unfamiliar with the texture of something that hasn't been boiled into paste."

Somebody at the next stall laughs under their breath, and I don't even have to look to know it's Earl Connelly. Old man's been selling sweet corn here since before I could walk, and he still hasn't forgiven me for poaching catfish out of his pond when I was fourteen. Earl's the type who can hold a grudge for decades and still offer you a bag of tomatoes on the house if he thinks you look too skinny.

"Don't mind me," he says, voice carrying over the baskets of produce. "Just enjoying the show."

I ignore him, but the corners of his mouth twitch like he's storing this up for his weekly visit to the hair salon. Earl's sister, Laverne, runs the crochet booth on the other side of the market, and if she's within earshot, half the county will know by Wednesday morning that Adam Williams was sparring with the *new French girl* over baked goods.

I keep my eyes on Christiane. She's flushed now, chin tilted, every inch of her daring me to keep going.

I set the jar down and pick up one of the scones. Still warm. Smells like peaches and spice. "This supposed to be ginger?"

"Yes," she says, sweet as arsenic. "It's good for the digestion."

I smirk. "What are you trying to say?"

She leans in just enough that I catch the faintest trace of flour and sugar on her skin. "Eat it and find out."

For a second, we just stare each other down. I'm not sure who's daring who more.

I pull a few bills from my wallet and drop them on the table. "I'll take the scone and the jam."

Her smile is all teeth. "Pleasure doing business with you."

The words are polite. The tone says *go step in manure.*

I turn away, but not far enough to lose sight of her.

A kid chasing a balloon nearly barrels into me, and I step aside, muttering to his mom that it's fine. Three stalls down, I stop at George's honey stand. He's got jars lined up like amber lanterns, beeswax candles stacked in pyramids.

"You sure you don't want a taste before you buy?" he asks.

"I'll take the wildflower," I say.

George glances toward Christiane's booth and smirks. "Or maybe you're already full from eating French scones."

"Mind your business," I mutter, handing him cash.

But Earl's watching from his corn stall, Laverne's pretending not to listen from behind her pile of crocheted baby blankets, and I know the whole damn market's filing this away.

I tell myself I'm just keeping an eye on the competition. But the scone in my bag is still warm, and I'm not tossing it to the pigs.

Chapter Five

Christiane

The market smells like sugar and sunlight.

Fried dough from the food truck by the gate, kettle corn popping in a copper kettle somewhere behind me, hay from the bales stacked as decoration for the harvest festival next month. There's a current of wood smoke in the air too; someone's running a grill. For just a moment, I let it all soak in, pretend it's the markets back home.

Not Paris, not even Marseille, but Provence.

The rhythm is the same: the hum of voices, the shuffle of baskets, vendors calling out specials in a singsong cadence that rises above the chatter. People linger, touch, and taste. Children dart between their legs. It's messy and alive and, if I squint past the accents and the curious looks, almost comforting.

Almost.

I arrive early on purpose, before the Saturday crowd thickens, so I can set my table exactly the way I want it. The green-checked cloth smooth and square, baskets lined like soldiers, chalkboard signs in crisp handwriting that took me far too long to perfect. Blackberry-Vanilla Jam. Peach-Ginger Scones. Lavender Shortbread. Loaves of bread dusted with flour so fine it looks like a breath of snow.

Every detail matters. Every straightened edge and careful placement is another brick in the wall I'm building between myself and the whispers. If I appear to belong, maybe I will eventually.

The sound of folding tables clanking into place drifts over from my left. A toddler shuffles past holding a pumpkin the size of his head, his father trailing behind with a bigger one under each arm. The boy's cheeks are flushed, his hair sticking up in the back, and he's holding the pumpkin like it's a treasure he dug from the earth himself. He catches sight of my scones, slows, and presses his small hand against the edge of my table like he's debating.

"Would you like one?" I ask gently. His eyes go wide, flicking to his father for permission.

The man nods. "Say thank you."

"Thank you," the boy mumbles, voice small but certain.

"You're very welcome." I hand him the smallest scone from the plate. His fingers brush mine, warm and sticky from something else he's eaten, and my throat tightens. It's nothing. Just a child. But I can't stop my mind from wandering to what it would be like to have someone look up at me like that every morning, to have a small hand reach for mine without hesitation.

I blink hard and busy myself with rearranging the basket of bread, pushing the thought back where it belongs. Wanting things you can't have is dangerous.

Mrs. Perry stops by before she opens her own stall, scanning my table like she's conducting an inspection. One of the crochet-and-gossip biddies, she rules the Wednesday morning hair salon like a general, but here, she plays market mayor.

"You should put bigger labels on those, dear," she says, squinting at my script. "Not everyone's been to France."

"Provence," I correct gently, pasting on the smile I reserve for interactions like this. "And I think most people can manage."

She chuckles, pats my arm, and wanders off, and I let my smile drop the second she turns away.

Comments like that are nothing on their own, but they pile up like pebbles in a shoe. You can walk through it, but eventually it bruises.

A shadow falls across my table, and I look up to see Nate Miller. Baseball cap tipped back, a bag of apples tucked under his arm, his smile is as easy as if we've been friends since childhood.

"These yours?" He nods toward the scones.

"They are." I offer him the sample plate.

He takes one bite, chews slowly like he's savoring it, and lets out a low whistle. "Best thing I've had all week. You make all this yourself?"

"I do. My mother taught me." Pride creeps into my voice before I can temper it.

"Well, my mom would've burned the kitchen down trying," he says with a grin. He hesitates, shifts the bag of apples under his arm. "Listen, have you ever eaten at the diner on Main? I was thinking... maybe Tuesday night? Dinner. Nothing fancy."

The invitation catches me off guard. My heart gives a foolish little kick.

"I... oh. I appreciate that," I manage.

"It's just dinner," he says with a shrug. "Unless you want it to be more. Could just be neighbors sharing a meal."

Neighbors.

That word lands heavier than it should. I'm not a neighbor here, not really. I'm the newcomer with the accent, the one whose name everyone says like it's too long for their mouths. Accepting feels like an invitation into something I'm not sure I'm allowed to have, belonging. And I've learned the hard way not to want things that can't last.

But Nate's grin is warm, and his eyes crinkle at the corners like he smiles often and means it.

"All right," I say finally. "Tuesday it is."

"Good." He tips his cap and heads off, disappearing into the crowd.

I'm still half smiling when I look up and freeze.

Adam Williams is at the far end of the row, talking to Earl Connelly, retired dairy farmer and sweet corn salesman, sporting a shirt as old as I am. Adam's wearing jeans and a faded T-shirt, sleeves pushed up, skin tanned from the sun. He belongs here in a way I never will, and I hate the way something in my chest stirs at the sight.

My spine straightens. I fuss with the sample plate. I don't look up.

The click of his boots gets closer, closer, until he's leaning against the edge of my table like he has every right to be there.

"Didn't realize you were running a charity," he says.

I blink at him. "Pardon?"

He nods toward my signs. "You're practically giving those away. Unless you plan on starving, I'd suggest charging what they're worth."

My chin tilts. "Thank you for your unsolicited business advice, Mr. Williams. How's that working out for you?"

"It's working fine. I'm not bankrupt yet." He picks up one of my jars, turning it in his hands like he's inspecting it for flaws. The glass is warm from the sun. "What's this supposed to be? Soup?"

My eyes narrow. "That's Blackberry-Vanilla Jam. Hand-picked berries. And no, it's not runny. You might be unfamiliar with the texture of something that hasn't been boiled into paste."

Someone at the next stall snorts, and I don't even have to glance sideways to know it's Earl. He lives for moments like this, a public poke at Adam, preferably with witnesses.

Adam smirks, sets the jar down, and picks up one of the scones. "This supposed to be ginger?"

"Yes," I say, sweet as arsenic. "It's good for the digestion."

"What are you trying to say?"

I lean in just enough to catch the smell of sunshine and hay from his shirt. "Eat it and find out."

For a second, we just stare each other down. I'm not sure who's daring who more.

He drops a few bills on the table. "I'll take the scone and the jam."

"Pleasure doing business with you," I say, my voice polite but my tone sharp enough to slice.

When he walks away, the tension doesn't leave with him. Instead, it lingers like the heat in the air, sparking whispers. The next hour is a blur of customers, some I recognize, some I've never seen before, all of them glancing toward where Adam went, some bold enough to ask if we've known each other long.

By the time the market starts to thin, I'm sold out of everything but two loaves of bread. The green-checked cloth is dusted with crumbs and sugar; my baskets are nearly empty.

Nate reappears, hands in his pockets, with that same easy smile. "Need a hand packing up?"

I laugh softly. "You really want to risk being demoted to jar boy?"

"Jar boy?" he echoes, mock offended. "That's a promotion. Let me help."

He doesn't wait for an answer; he just scoops up a crate and carries it as if it weighs nothing. We fall into step, moving back and forth between table and truck, teasing each other about who's slower, who stacked the jars better, who almost tripped over the curb. It's light, effortless, and by the time the last crate is loaded, I'm smiling more than I mean to.

He leans against the tailgate once we're finished, wiping his hands on his jeans. "See? No pulled muscles. All thanks to me."

"Thank you," I say, meaning it more than I should.

"Tuesday," he reminds me, tipping his cap before heading off toward his own truck.

I climb into my cab, the heat of the day finally catching up with me.

And that's when I see him.

Adam, leaning against the hood of his truck across the lot, a jar of honey in one hand, watching. Not moving. Not smiling. Just watching.

My chest tightens, though whether it's anger or something else, I can't tell. I turn the key in the ignition and pull away, forcing myself not to look back.

Even so, I feel his gaze burning into me all the way down Main Street.

Chapter Six

Adam

The morning is already off-kilter. I'm halfway to the barn to meet the vet about Reggie's hoof when I realize the bull isn't where he's supposed to be. A missing bull is never a good surprise. The holding pen tells the story: wire sagging, post leaning, dirt churned fresh. He didn't wander. He made a choice.

A burst of French cuts through the air, furious, sharp enough to sting. "Adam! Get your cow away from me before he does something!"

I round the lilacs and stop cold. Christiane is pinned on her porch, flour on her cheek, braid slipping loose. She's clutching a tray of cinnamon twists, steam rising in the morning air. Reggie has planted himself on her steps, nosing toward the smell. The boards groan under his weight.

"Bull," I correct, moving fast. "And he doesn't eat people."

"How am I supposed to know that?" she snaps. "He looks like he eats everything."

"Not everything. Easy, Reggie. Back up."

He doesn't. He stretches higher, velvet lips brushing the pan. Christiane jerks it up, pressing back into the jamb.

Then Emmanuel barrels across the yard, ears flat, head down—a battering ram of bad decisions. He bounces off Reggie like a rubber ball, lands in basil, and rears up to scream as if physics personally betrayed him.

"Idiot," Christiane gasps. "Absolute idiot."

Duke bounds in late, barking at exactly the wrong times. Reggie flicks an ear, shifting. The porch creaks loudly.

"Duke, heel," I bark. He plants his butt, vibrating with pride, as if sitting still fixed everything. I take the stairs at a clip, putting myself between her and the bull. Up close, Reggie radiates heat. Cinnamon clings to the air, fear just beneath it. Behind me, Christiane is close enough that I can smell lavender underneath the scent of cinnamon twists.

"Open the door," I say low. "Set the tray inside."

Her eyes stay locked on Reggie. "I'm not turning my back on him."

"Then do it while I'm here." Turning to block Reggie's view, I brace one hand on the jamb beside her head. Her pulse jumps in her throat. Mine answers. "I've got him." I swallow roughly, staring down at her. I'm close enough to see the freckles that dust across her nose.

She opens the door with fingers that only shake a little. The tray clinks onto the counter inside. She steps back out, chin high again, as if nothing happened in that breath between us.

"Good," I murmur before turning back to face Reggie. "Back up, big man. Not yours."

I reach out to grab him, and the halter creaks under my grip as Reggie tests me. Emmanuel ricochets off his fetlock into the geraniums. Dirt flies. Duke barks at it.

"Christ, that goat is going to get himself killed," I mutter. "Back, Reggie. Back."

Finally, Reggie shifts, one step then two, head lowering. I stroke the ridge between his eyes. "Good. C'mon. Let's go home. You've got a doctor coming to see you."

"Don't talk to him like he's a puppy. Don't make him look cute." Christiane says, voice thinner now.

"Five minutes and a grain bucket, he'll be penned. Then it will all be over." Reggie sneezes, sliming her welcome mat. She yelps. Laughter claws at my chest. I swallow it down.

"It's not funny," she says.

"It's a little funny."

I guide Reggie down the steps. He snorts once at Emmanuel, who screams in defiance from the steps, then lets me lead him back across the pasture.

By the time I shut the gate, Doc's truck is pulling in.

"Morning," he says, eyeing my mud-smeared jeans. "Looks like cardio."

"He found religion," I mutter, "and Cinnamon."

Doc laughs, checks the hoof. "Sole bruise. Tender, not bad. Keep him on dry ground a couple of days."

"Copy."

While he packs up, my mind's already on the sagging fence line and the scuff on her porch rail.

"You want me to explain bull behavior to her?" Doc asks.

"That's my job," I say too quickly. He grins, hearing what I didn't say.

When he's gone, I fix the post and rail before she can call Paul the contractor. She opens the door partway as I work, the aroma of cinnamon spilling out. Sugar dust clings to her apron, one streak of flour she missed is by her temple. She doesn't wipe it.

"I can call Paul," she says.

"I'm here," I answer. "And it was my bull."

She hesitates, pride warring with relief. "Fine. Thank you."

"You're welcome."

Her gaze flicks to Emmanuel skulking by the rosemary. "He thinks he's ten feet tall."

"Four hooves and an opinion." The laugh that breaks from her is quick, real. It hits me hard.

When I'm done, sweat sticking to my shirt, she leans on the doorframe, watching. "You do that fast."

"Ranching's just fixing and breaking in circles," I say.

"I'm learning." Her voice hitches. "Thank you."

The words land heavier this time. I nod before Duke drops a rope at my feet, and Emmanuel tries to steal it. Christiane snorts, covers her mouth, then lets it drop.

"I'll run hot wire after lunch," I say, breaking the moment before it takes me somewhere dangerous.

Inside, the brothers are at the table, mugs in hand. Eli trails hay, Patrick looks calm as always, and Brandon smirks.

"Reggie got out," I say, pouring coffee. "Pinned Christiane at the door. Cinnamon twists are now contraband."

Brandon snorts. "Bull's got taste."

"It's not funny," I say, though my mouth twitches. "The post was rotten. I braced it. Hot wire this afternoon. Get me two treated posts, clips, and the stretcher."

"You want help or you want it done right?" Brandon grins.

"Bring the damn stretcher."

Eli snags a biscuit. "Emmanuel try to kill him?"

"Repeatedly."

Eli cackles. "Little man's got more heart than sense."

Patrick looks at me over his mug. "Not the only one."

"What?"

"Nothing. Just saying, you came in jaw tight, like a man looking for a fight he doesn't want."

"The fight's the fence," I snap.

"Good," Patrick says evenly. "Because if we're bringing in Stewart calves this fall, we need more ground or a thinner herd. Rotations are already packed."

"If Morrison had sold like he was supposed to, we wouldn't be talking about this," I mutter.

"He didn't," Patrick replies. "So we cut bulls, rent ground, or ask her about grazing rights on the back five."

The words hit like a slap. Her land. My jaw tightens.

"Not happening."

Patrick tilts his head. "Because you don't want to ask, or because you don't want to owe her?"

"Yes."

They laugh. I don't.

"We'll figure acres," Brandon says, rising. "I'll grab the stretcher. Eli, posts. Patrick, referee if Adam starts lecturing the goat again."

"Goat needs structure," I grumble.

"I'm ungovernable," Eli shoots back.

Patrick claps his shoulder on the way out. "Don't forget staples this time."

"I forgot once," Eli protests.

"Three times."

Their noise fades, leaving me at the table, palms flat, staring at the shared fence line. From here, I can see the edge of her porch. If I let myself, I could believe I still smell sugar in the air.

I tell myself the knot in my chest is logistics—acres, rotations, wire. Easier to believe that than admit the truth: her voice wrapping around my name, her laugh breaking loose, the way it felt when she let me stand as her wall.

I grab my hat. There's wire to pull, a bull to pen, and a line I need to remember exists—no matter how often my feet cross it.

Chapter Seven
Christiane

I'm running late because of a button.

One tiny pearl circle refuses to slip through its loop while my hands wobble like I've never dressed myself before. I take a breath, steady my fingers, and coax it into place. The blouse settles against my skin, cream in the lamp glow. I smooth the fabric and tell myself I'm not nervous.

I am.

I haven't done this in a long time—meeting someone for dinner, close enough to smell their soap, to answer questions that peel back layers. A date, even if he said it didn't have to be one. My stomach doesn't know the difference.

In the mirror, I tug my hair into a knot, wipe a streak of flour off my jaw from this afternoon's test batch, and dab perfume behind my ears. Orange flower. Vanilla. A ghost of home. *Maman* always said a touch of scent was like a promise to yourself.

Emmanuel bleats by the back door as if he approves, then knocks his horns against the wood. "*Du calme, mon démon*," I call, shrugging into my coat. "I will not be gone long."

He stares through the window—judgmental, fond, rude—a perfect goat. Daisy and Dandie lift their heads from the hay. Cookie blinks solemnly. Leaving them feels like sneaking out of a house full of children.

Outside, the cold is clean and bright, stars pressing close. Gravel crunches under my boots. The porch still smells faintly of cinnamon from the rolls I iced an hour ago.

Nate waits at the end of the drive, hands in his jacket pockets, a grin crinkling his eyes. He looks just as he did at the market—open, warm, steady. "Evening," he says. "You look—uh—nice."

"Thank you." Heat rises in my cheeks. "You do too."

We fall into step, cutting across a path through the pasture. The grass snaps underfoot. Somewhere, a fox yips. Nate tells me about pruning trees after frost, about his mother's rule never to trim on a waning moon. Superstition or science, he doesn't care, as long as the apples come sweet.

I like the way he talks. Not to impress, just to share. When he asks about the diner, I hear myself describing the dreams I've only whispered to the walls: fresh bread every morning, a pastry case that glows at dawn, coffee made like someone cares if you wake up kind.

"That sounds like a place I'd want to sit in," he says.

"Me too," I admit. The words leave something tender exposed.

Main Street glows ahead. Florist windows spill light. Maggie's Diner hums in neon red, the For Sale sign taped to the glass. My chest lurches—hope or terror, I can't tell.

Inside, warmth rolls over us along with the scents of coffee, onions, and lemon cleaner. The bell jingles. Maggie calls from the counter, "Well, look at you, Ms. Fancy Eggs. Sit anywhere."

We slide into a corner booth. Nate orders meatloaf and a milkshake. I order roast chicken; comfort on a plate.

"Wine?" he asks, glancing at the chalkboard where someone's written *Merlot* in optimistic chalk.

I shake my head. "Not with Maggie's food. Coffee's better."

"You're a woman after my own heart."

I ask about his orchard. He asks about bread. The talk settles into an easy rhythm I haven't felt in years. Then a toddler at the counter drops a fork. The clatter makes me flinch. He looks at me like I can fix it. I smile and wave. The ache that follows is sharp and familiar.

Nate notices. "You like kids?"

"Yes." The word is thin. I clear my throat. "Very much."

"Me too." He leans back. "Someday I'd like a pack of them, running wild between the trees."

The picture is sweet, almost too sweet. But in my mind, another voice curls around my name at night, one that isn't his.

Dinner arrives, steaming. We eat, trading small stories. I confess that a raccoon once stole a cinnamon roll right off my windowsill while staring me down. Nate laughs so hard he nearly cries. For a moment, the ache eases.

Later, over half-cold coffee, he asks, "Do you miss it? France?"

"I miss the people," I say carefully. "Being understood without trying. But land is land—stubborn and generous in any language. I can build here too."

"I think you will," he says simply. And I believe he means it.

We pay. Maggie winks, warning me not to trust anyone who skips breakfast. I tuck it away like a charm.

Outside, the night sharpens. Across the street, a truck idles in the shadows. A man leans against the fender, arms crossed, head tipped. For one second, I pretend I don't see him. Then I look. Adam doesn't move. Doesn't wave. He just watches, expression unreadable.

"You okay?" Nate asks.

"Cold," I lie.

We walk on. A woman sweeping the florist's steps pretends not to watch us pass. This town is a choir; gossip is the hymn.

At the fork in the road, Nate hesitates. "Can I see you again? Next Thursday, maybe? Brick-oven pizza in Sycamore?"

I should say no. I want to say yes. A second chance at easy feels like something I should take.

"Yes," I hear myself say.

His smile blooms. He kisses my cheek, polite and careful, leaving the door open without pushing through. I'm grateful for that.

When he turns toward the orchard, I linger. Across from the diner, the truck eases into gear and disappears. Duke's ears vanish last.

On the walk home, the cold finds every seam in my coat. At the porch, Emmanuel bleats once. I press my hand to his head.

"It was nice," I tell him. "He is nice."

He tries to eat my scarf.

Inside, the kitchen smells of sugar. Cinnamon rolls gleam on the counter. I break one in half, sugar crumbling. *Maman* would say I'm feeding something that isn't hunger. I eat anyway.

In the mirror, I practice not looking toward the road. In bed, the sheets are cold and honest. The last thing I hear before sleep is the wind asking the same question Emmanuel did without words.

What now?

I pull the blanket up to my chin and think: keep going. Build the thing. Be brave. Don't look for him across the street.

I fail at the last one before morning.

Chapter Eight

Adam

Duke paces before the sun crests the horizon, nails clicking a restless rhythm on the old wood floor. I tug on my boots, shove the door open, and he bolts. Frost bites at the grass, sharp and temporary, the kind that cuts while it lasts but will be gone by midmorning.

This should be the best part of the day. Quiet. Clean. Uncomplicated.

But it's not. Not since she showed up.

I walk the fence line like I always do, scanning the rails, listening for the telltale groan of warped wood or the soft drag of something loose. Routine's supposed to settle me. Keep the noise in my head at bay. But today it's useless.

Because I hear her.

Her voice drifts across the field, low and lilting. French. She's crouched in her yard, murmuring to Emmanuel like they're partners in crime. He bleats, she laughs, and the sound punches right through me. That laugh—warm, unguarded—makes this place feel like something it hasn't in a long time. Alive.

I grit my teeth and turn back to work.

I toss myself into chores. Stalls. Tack. Hay. Anything to keep my hands busy. But it doesn't clear her from my head. She's there in every rhythm, every hammer strike. Like a song I can't stop humming.

Then Duke barks. Not his regular bark. This one's sharp. High. Urgent.

A second later, her shriek cuts through the air.

My stomach drops. I run.

By the time I round the corner, Christiane's perched on a stack of hay bales, clutching a box of chicks to her chest like a shield. Duke's below, tail wagging, barking like he's discovered the meaning of life. She's yelling into her phone, a tangle of French and English spilling out as her eyes dart between the dog and the trembling box.

"Christiane!" I shout, striding fast. "What the hell's going on?"

She swings her glare to me, hair coming loose around her face, cheeks flushed. "Your dog tried to eat my chicks!"

"He's not trying to eat them," I snap back, pulling Duke to my side. "He's a livestock guardian. He thinks they're his flock."

Her chin lifts, sharp as a blade. "Flock? He is barking like he wants them for breakfast."

Duke gives another high-pitched bark and hops up against the bale. She wobbles, boots scraping straw, the box tipping dangerously. Instinct takes over; I lunge, catching her around the waist. The box presses between us, her breath stuttering against my neck. For a heartbeat, we're locked together. Too close. She smells like sugar and citrus, her hair brushing my jaw. I feel her tremble, though she tries to hide it.

Then she jerks back, cheeks flushed crimson.

"Let him sniff them," I say, trying to sound calm while my pulse pounds. "He'll stop barking."

She hesitates, lips pressed tight, then lowers the box an inch. Duke sniffs, huffs, and loses interest, trotting off like the whole show's beneath him now.

"See?" I smirk. "Menace averted."

She glares like she'd like to throttle me. "He's still trouble."

"Welcome to ranch life, sweetheart."

Before she can fire back, gravel crunches. A sheriff's cruiser pulls in, lights off, and Sheriff Harris leans against the hood, his mouth twitching. "Morning, Adam. Got yourself a crisis?"

I rub my temple. "False alarm."

Christiane mutters something sharp in French and storms inside, chicks still hugged to her chest like precious cargo. The sheriff chuckles, tips his hat, and drives off. Duke barks once, as if proud of himself, before flopping in the dirt.

That afternoon, I head up my own porch steps and freeze. Emmanuel's halfway through my screen door, chewing on the mesh like it's a delicacy.

"You've got to be kidding me."

Christiane barrels around the corner, breathless. "Emmanuel! Get out of there!"

I cross my arms, leaning against the doorframe. "Lose something?"

She flushes, cheeks pink. "He got out. I don't know how."

"He's got a homing instinct—for my house."

Without missing a beat, she ducks past me, wafting citrus and sugar as she storms into my living room like she belongs there. Emmanuel trots happily after her.

"You planning to wrangle him or redecorate with hoof-prints?" I call after her.

"You could help," she snaps, hair falling loose as she lunges for the goat.

"You seem to have a system."

She dives. Emmanuel dodges. Straight into me. Again. She stumbles, and I catch her. Again. Her hands land on my chest. Eyes wide. Lips parted. For a moment, everything goes quiet. Too close. Way too close.

"You really gotta stop throwing yourself at me," I murmur, my voice low and rough.

Her lips twitch almost into a smile, nearly a spark, but then Emmanuel bleats and bolts toward the kitchen. She pulls away fast. "I should… get him," she mutters.

I nod, watching her go, the heat still crawling under my skin. Yeah. This isn't over. Not by a long shot.

Chapter Nine

Christiane

Emmanuel is screaming like he's being murdered.

I sprint outside, boots half laced, sweater crooked, breath burning cold in my throat. Morning light is thin and blue, frost sugaring the grass. He's tangled in the wire by the barn, legs kicking, eyes wild.

"Oh, *mon dieu*," I whisper, dropping to my knees. "*Doucement, mon démon*. Be still."

The wire bites my palms as I work fast, fingers numb. I pin his shoulder with my arm, not hard, just steady. Back leg first, then front, easing loops from his ankle. When the last slip frees, he springs up in one furious hop, trembling, glaring at the world like it betrayed him.

"You're fine," I say, voice shaking. "Drama king."

He butts my shoulder as if I were the problem all along. I huff out a laugh and turn to the fence.

Third time this week.

The break isn't rot—it's clean. A staple pried just enough to slacken the wire. Too neat to be weather. Not an accident.

A boot print dents the soil near the corner post, bigger than mine, fresh. My stomach goes tight. Papa Mark's voice echoes: *People test what you claim, ma fille. Walk your line every night.*

I finish the repair and lead Emmanuel to the pen. He trots to hay as if none of it happened. I envy him.

Inside, silence hums too loudly. I bake scones I don't want, just to put butter and cinnamon in the air. When the timer dings, I open one, watch steam curl, taste nothing. My phone buzzes. Meeting with Paul Turner at ten.

It took a month to get on his calendar. Waiting meant I was still here. Waiting meant time passed.

Paul is already on the porch when I arrive in town, pencil tucked behind his ear.

"Morning, Christiane," he says warmly. "How are you settling in?"

"I am. Mostly. There are hiccups."

He gestures toward Main. "Let's look at the diner first."

Maggie's sign glows red. The bell jingles as we step inside. Coffee, grease, lemon cleaner—layers that smell like morning. Cracked tiles. A sulking jukebox.

"You still set on making this place sing?" Maggie asks, pouring coffee.

"I am," I say, steadier than expected. "Fresh floors. A hood. Espresso. A pastry case that shows off."

Paul checks under sinks, opens cabinets, and taps the breaker. "Old, but serviceable. Replace the hood; we update to the latest code. Floors need tile. Cosmetics later. Walk-in's fine for now."

"Watch what you're calling old," Maggie says. "This place is held together by prayer and bacon fat."

"Prayer I have. Bacon fat I can borrow."

Paul scribbles notes. "Staff?"

"I'll bake, run the front. Then hire a cook and server. Budget's tight. We'll phase."

"That works," he nods. "Start with safety. You paint, you'll save."

Maggie slides muffins toward me. "She'll work harder than anyone you know."

"I can see that," Paul murmurs.

He promises an estimate in days, then, "Let's see your porch."

Crossing the square, I feel eyes. Mrs. Talbot whispers behind her hand. Jake nods from the feed store.

And then Adam steps out of the hardware store, rope over his shoulder, sunlight catching the stubble that makes him look like he's already fought the day and won. Patrick's behind him. Brandon's across the street with coffee.

The square stills.

"Morning," Patrick says.

"Morning," I answer.

Adam's eyes flick to Paul's clipboard. His voice carries without raising. "Seems like you're buying up half of Main Street."

Heat climbs my cheeks. "Exactly one thing. The one with a For Sale sign."

People slow. Maggie leans in her doorway, eyebrow arched.

"Hope you brought enough money for the upkeep," Adam says. "Houses out here eat more than goats."

"Then it's good thing I can bake. I hear biscuits pay bills."

Brandon snorts. Patrick shoots him a warning look. The square exhales.

Paul clears his throat. "I'll meet you at the truck."

I nod, spine straight, and turn away.

Back at the farm, Paul walks me through sagging beams, loose tin, and fence lines. When I tell him about the cut wire, his gaze sharpens. He crouches, finds another pried staple I'd missed.

"Deliberate," he says. "Reinforce the posts. Consider a trail cam—even a fake one."

"I don't want to be the woman who installs cameras," I mutter.

"You want to be the woman who is safe," he replies gently.

Gratitude tastes safer than fear. "Thank you."

When his truck pulls away, the quiet falls thinner than before.

That's when Adam's engine comes.

He parks by the road, walks along my fence as if it belongs to him. Emmanuel prances past with a stolen towel.

"You planning to fix that corner?" Adam calls.

"I did. Twice."

"It's still cracked."

"You think?"

I step down, towel in hand. Our fingers brush as we both reach. Warmth jolts through me. He lets go first.

"That one's going to be trouble," he says, nodding at Emmanuel. His mouth almost smiles.

"He already is," I answer. "Persistent. Scrappy. Doesn't know when to quit."

"Sounds familiar."

We stand with the fence between us, a line thin as breath.

Finally, I say it. "I could use another set of eyes. Someone's cutting staples. Tomorrow morning? Before chores?"

He studies me, then nods. "Dawn. Bring a hammer."

"I have one."

"I figured." His voice is almost warm. "I'll bring staples."

"Thank you," I whisper.

He tips his chin, heads for his truck. "Keep the goat off my porch."

"You keep yours from smelling like biscuits," I shoot back, half a joke, half something else.

His hand lifts once; the movement small but still too big. Then he's gone.

I walk the fence again, fingertips grazing staples, slow and deliberate, as if touch alone could hold the line.

Tomorrow, I'll walk it with him. That's either nothing or the beginning of something I can't yet name.

Chapter Ten

Adam

Duke starts pacing before dawn, nails clicking on the old wood floor. A soft whine says the day is already late and I'm the only one who doesn't know it.

I pull on jeans and a flannel, step into the cold that bites like it means it. Frost skins the grass, thin and white, catching the early blue light like sugar. Our houses sit closer than I'd like—one hundred and fifty yards, a shared fence between us. Four-rail pine, barbed top and bottom, a pipe gate chained but never locked. For emergencies. For neighbors. I never thought I'd be using it to keep a goat out.

Duke and I walk the line. He noses rails; I check for sag and split. At the elm, the bottom rail bows where Emmanuel wriggled through last week. I patched it with a scrap of field wire and a rock. Temporary, but it'll do until Paul Turner brings new posts.

Her voice drifts over the fog—French, soft and steady, like steam on a winter window. The breeze shifts, carrying the scent of butter and sugar. Peach and ginger. My mouth remembers the scone I bought at the market, eaten behind Earl's corn truck like it was contraband. I keep walking. Fence, latch, post. The rhythm usually steadies me. Today, it just reminds me she's there.

By sunup, I'm buried in chores. Hay fork, troughs, sweep the aisle. Check Reggie's fetlock—sound now, full of himself, banging the panels for a treat. I don't give him one.

Inside, Brandon is stirring oatmeal that smells like punishment. Patrick leans against the doorway, calm as a priest.

"You look better than yesterday," Patrick says.

"Fence held. Cold tightened it up."

Brandon smirks. "Or maybe the goat's moved on to knitting. Heard you've got a new hobby yourself."

Patrick sighs. "Just say it."

Brandon grins. "Word in town is you bought a scone."

I keep my face blank. "I was hungry."

"Hungry enough to hide behind Earl's truck?" Patrick coughs on his coffee. Brandon looks like Christmas came early.

"It was research," I mutter.

Brandon laughs because we all know the truth.

We run down the day's work—west well, auction house, feed. But what fills my head isn't chores. It's Christiane in Maggie's Diner yesterday, standing with Paul Turner, pointing at ceiling joists and pastry cases like she already saw the place remade in her head. She wasn't trying it on like a whim. She was building. And damn if I didn't want to stand there listening.

I shove the thought away and work until the sun goes long and gold. It's the hour my grandfather loved, when the fence lines glow and cattle stand easy. Legacy hour. The kind of light that makes you believe all the sacrifices will add up to something. I open the ledger, but the neat lines blur. Papa's notes in the back pages look like they belong to a man softer than me.

The door slams open. Eli barrels in, grin wide.

"What did you break?" I ask.

"Nothing." Which always means something.

Patrick watches him steadily, already bracing.

Eli shrugs. "Stopped by the Frenchwoman's

His jaw sets. "It was a joke."

"It's not a joke if an animal gets out. Not a joke if she thinks place with some friends. Nudged a few boards. Knocked over her mailbox. Nothing big. Just enough to make her wonder."

My chair scrapes back. He startles.

"You did what?"

"You said she doesn't belong. I was helping."

"You were trespassing," I snap. "And a coward. A pack of boys pushing over a mailbox; do you really think that will make you a man? You break one board, a steer gets hit the road at two a.m., that blood's on you."

His face reddens.

"You'll fix the boards. You'll stand her mailbox straight. You'll knock on her door and tell her it won't happen again."

"I'm not—"

"You are," I say, and the tone makes him flinch. "You live under this roof, you carry my name, you don't get to be a bully. Not here. Not ever. Not to her."

He storms out. The silence after is loud.

"You gonna tell her it was him?" Patrick asks.

"No. I'll make sure it never happens again."

That night, frost creeps back over the pasture. Duke follows as I carry cut rails and a pocket of screws down to the elm. My headlamp throws a weak circle of light. Breath smokes, fingers burn, but I work until the gap is solid. Not pretty. Not permanent. Enough.

Her kitchen window glows. A shadow shifts. For one beat, I think about knocking. About telling her Eli's an idiot. About telling her she can sleep tonight.

I don't.

I stand with my hand on the rail, cold, biting bone. Legacy was supposed to be the answer—acre by acre, fence by fence. But then she showed up and baked something that tasted like a life I didn't plan for.

Back inside, bourbon burns down my throat. Duke curls under my chair. The clock ticks too loudly. Outside, the land holds its breath.

I glance toward the window one last time. Her light is still on.

I tell myself it doesn't matter.

But I know it does.

Chapter Eleven

Christiane

The mailbox is on its side again.

"*Merde*," I mutter, squatting to lift it. The pole is bent now, leaning at an angle no amount of willpower will fix. I fish my gloves from my apron pocket, set the box upright in its broken cradle, and try not to think about how many times I've done this.

I'll need a new post. Maybe concrete. Maybe a miracle.

The wind shifts. Morning sun glints over the pasture, catching on dew that clings to the grass. It's beautiful. Soft. If I squint, it almost looks like home. Not Willow Glen. France. Before everything broke.

Papa Mark and I used to walk the fence lines at this hour, coffee mugs in hand, *Maman*'s cinnamon rolls waiting inside. The memory crests warm, then sharp. It hurts in the way old grief always does—sudden and familiar.

I gather the damp mail from the grass—mostly ads, one water bill—and head inside. The screen door slams shut behind me. The silence in the house presses in, too thick and full of unsaid things. I set the mail on the counter and go straight out to the coop.

The hens cluck and bustle at the sound of the latch. These aren't the chicks from weeks ago—they're nowhere near ready. These came from Jake at the feed store, pulled from a neighbor's extra flock. "Hardy layers, just hitting their stride," he'd promised, and he was right.

"*Bonjour, mes poules!* Do you have some lovely gifts for me this morning?" My voice is too bright, too forced, but they don't mind. They crowd around my boots, feathers brushing my ankles, scratching and pecking as if I'm royalty.

The air is warm inside the coop, heavy with the musk of straw, feed, and that faint mineral tang of fresh eggs. I kneel to collect them, running my fingers over their smooth shells, still radiating the warmth of the hen's body.

"Paisley, you're a queen. That's a perfect blue egg. Beatrice—*non*! Buckets are not nests. Melanie—ow! Stop it, or you're dinner, I swear."

A laugh slips out despite myself. It feels like something breaking loose inside me, a place grief hasn't fully cemented shut.

I tuck the eggs into the basket and carry them to the goats. The moment I open the gate, Emmanuel makes a break for it.

"Emmanuel!" I shout, but he's already lunging for the feed bucket. His teeth clamp on the handle like a bandit caught red-handed.

"Ugh, non—you little gremlin, give it back!"

We wrestle. He wins. He always wins. Tail flicking, he prances in triumph across the yard, swinging the bucket like a trophy.

"You're evil," I mutter, hands on my hips. He bleats, smug as a king.

Daisy, Dandie, and Debbie wait patiently at the milking stand, far better citizens. I brush each one before milking, the rhythm soothing me: pull, release, sigh of milk into the pail. Not everything in my life is broken. Some things still work if you keep showing up for them.

But the peace never lasts long. I spot Emmanuel again—head poking around the barn, eyes too smart for his own good.

"Emmanuel..." I warn.

He vanishes. Trouble for later.

Inside, I strain the milk and clean up, though the kitchen feels colder than usual. Too clean. Too quiet. I set the dough to rise and keep busy, but when the rolls collapse in the pan, the sting is sharper than it should be. It's just dough. But everything already feels fragile, and this is the last crack.

The scent of cinnamon fills the house anyway. Sweet. Heavy. Almost too much to bear.

Then, a movement outside catches my eye. A white blur streaks across the grass.

"Are you kidding me?"

I storm onto the porch.

"Duke! Go home!"

Adam's damn dog stops by the chicken coop, tail wagging furiously. When he sees me, he flops belly-up in the grass, tongue lolling like I'm the best thing that's ever happened to him.

"Duke," I groan. "You do not live here. Don't give me those eyes. I'm not rubbing your belly. I mean it."

He blinks, shameless.

"I will not rub your belly," I repeat. I rub his belly.

The traitor pants happily, kicking one leg like a windmill.

"You're so lucky you're cute," I mutter. "Your owner is a pain in my ass, but you had to have puppy dog eyes. Literal ones."

I wonder, not for the first time, if Duke comes because he wants to, or because Adam knows exactly how much it rattles me to have his dog lying across my porch like he belongs.

Later that afternoon, a knock jolts me. I wipe flour from my hands and crack the door. Eli Williams stands on the porch, a brand-new mailbox post balanced on one shoulder, tools in hand.

He shifts awkwardly. "Uh. I brought this."

I blink. "That's... unexpected."

"Yeah, well. I messed with the last one. Thought it was funny. It wasn't. Adam set me straight."

I cross my arms. "So this is an apology?"

"Yeah. Kind of." He scratches his jaw. "Can I fix it? Got the stuff in the truck."

I hesitate, then nod. "Fine. Go ahead."

He gets to work silently, digging, setting, leveling, his movements efficient. The scent of raw cedar blends with the damp earth. I bring him lemonade because that's what you do here, apparently, and he takes it with a grunt.

"Look, I was being a jerk," he says finally. "The guys and I thought if we made things annoying, you'd just leave."

"And now?"

He shrugs. "Now I think you're more stubborn than the rest of us. And Adam's serious. You don't want to be on the wrong side of him when he's mad."

A laugh escapes me. "No, I don't suppose I do."

Eli looks embarrassed, almost sheepish. "Anyway. Sorry. For real. You've got guts. That counts around here."

When he finishes, the mailbox stands straighter than it ever has. Solid. Rooted. Like it belongs.

I disappear into the kitchen, return with a paper plate wrapped in foil. "Here. Cinnamon rolls. Peace offering."

His eyes widen. "You didn't have to."

"I know. But I wanted to."

He takes them, nodding once. "Guess we're good, then."

"Yeah," I say softly. "We're good."

When he leaves, I linger at the end of the walk. The sun slants low across the new post, the scent of cinnamon still clinging to my clothes. For the first time in weeks, something eases in my chest.

Maybe, just maybe, things are starting to change.

Chapter Twelve

Adam

I step out onto the back porch and stretch, rolling my shoulders until something pops. A new body part aches every damn morning, but it comes with the job. This life—this land—is all I've ever known. It's not glamorous, but it's mine. Has been for generations.

I sip from my mug and take in the view: cattle grazing in the pasture, rows of crops catching the first light like brushed gold. It should feel like peace.

But it doesn't.

Because Duke isn't at my feet where he should be.

By the time I whistle, he's already loping back from the direction of the Devereaux place, tongue lolling, tail swishing like he's done something heroic. His fur smells faintly of cinnamon and sugar. There's even a dusting of flour across his shoulder like somebody swatted him away from a mixing bowl.

I scrub a hand over my jaw. "You traitor," I mutter. "You'd sell me out for baked goods."

He pants happily, flops at my boots, and rolls to his back. Not a care in the world. Meanwhile, I can't shake the picture forming in my head—Christiane in her kitchen, apron floured, muttering in French while she shoos him out the door.

And the worst part? My damn dog looks happier over there.

I down the rest of my coffee and head inside before I think too hard about it.

Brandon's at the stove, spatula in hand, bacon popping in the skillet. Patrick's already at the table with his coffee, reading something on his phone. They both glance up when I walk in, and I can see it—the grins they're trying not to let loose.

"Don't," I warn, dropping into a chair.

"Didn't say a word," Brandon says, way too fast.

Patrick lowers his mug. "You look restless. More than usual."

"Fence still needs work," I mutter. "West side's holding for now, but I don't trust it. Cows need to be shifted closer to the barn and calves separated soon. Ain't time to be worrying about anything else."

"Mm-hm," Patrick says, voice like he doesn't believe a word.

Brandon grins at the skillet. "Sure that's all it is? Nothing to do with why Duke came home smelling like a bakery?"

My head snaps up. "What?"

He smirks. "Flour on his fur. Sugar in the air. Unless you're hiding a side hustle, I'd say he's been hanging around your new neighbor."

"Christiane's not my neighbor," I snap. "She's a squatter with paperwork."

Patrick sets his mug down with a deliberate thunk. "She's not squatting, Adam. She bought the Morrison place fair and square. Paperwork counts more than your temper."

I glare at him. He doesn't blink.

Brandon just grins wider. "If she keeps feeding Duke, you're gonna lose custody."

"Not funny," I mutter.

Patrick shrugs. "Looked funny from where I'm sitting."

Before I can fire back, the front door creaks open and Eli strolls in like he owns the place. He's got the mail in one hand and a pastry in the other—cinnamon frosting smeared across his mouth like war paint.

"These cinnamon rolls are insane," he announces around a mouthful. "Best I've ever had. Christiane sure can bake."

I pinch the bridge of my nose. "Please tell me you didn't beg food off her."

"I didn't ask," Eli says, grinning like the cat that ate the canary. "I went to fix her mailbox. You told me to make it right, remember? She gave me these as a thank-you. Guess that means we're square now."

Patrick coughs into his mug. Brandon snorts into the skillet.

"You're not supposed to be making friends with her," I growl.

"Why not?" Eli shrugs, licking frosting off his thumb. "She's nice. A bit high-strung. But honestly, I kinda like her."

"You would," I mutter.

"Better than you glaring at her like she's the devil," Eli smirks. "Maybe if you tried one of these, you'd relax." He waves half a cinnamon roll at me. Brandon makes a grab for it, but Eli dodges like he's guarding treasure.

Patrick just shakes his head. "Maggie was talking in town. Word is that Christiane's definitely buying her diner. Folks seemed excited about it."

I stiffen. "You sure?"

"Yep," Patrick says. "Apparently, contracts are moving along. People are saying it's about time someone breathed new life into the place. Maggie's thrilled to hand it to a baker."

Brandon flips the bacon with a grin. "Sounds like half the town's rooting for her."

I don't answer. Can't. The thought of her planting roots deeper here—claiming more than just the farm—scrapes at every raw edge I've got.

Eli polishes off the last bite of pastry with a satisfied groan. "If she starts selling these in town, you're all gonna be out of luck. I'll move in over there and eat breakfast every morning."

"Over my dead body," I snap.

He blinks, caught off guard by my tone. Patrick studies me, quiet and sharp-eyed, and Brandon smirks like he's won something.

I shove back from the table, scraping the chair loudly against the floor. "I'm heading into Willow Glen Feed. Anyone needs me, that's where I'll be."

Brandon calls after me, "Pick up some cinnamon while you're at it!"

The door slams behind me before I can answer.

By the time I pull into town, Willow Glen's already stirring. Shopkeepers prop open their doors. Flower boxes spill color down Main Street. And everywhere I go, I hear her name.

"Christiane's really doing it—buying Maggie's place."

"She's got big plans for the diner."

"About time that place had some life again."

Each word digs deeper, settling like burrs under my skin. I keep my head down, grab the feed I came for, and get the hell out before someone asks my opinion.

But even back on my porch, sack of feed slung over my shoulder, the smell of cinnamon still clings in the air. Haunting me.

Chapter Thirteen
Christiane

The moment I step into Willow Glen Feed, I inhale deeply and slowly. Hay, grain, leather—it smells like rhythm, like purpose, like the shape of a life I'm still trying to rebuild.

I grab a red plastic basket from the stack by the door and wander the aisles. A sack of grit goes in first, then mineral blocks, then a bag of scratch grain that's almost too heavy for the flimsy basket. Emmanuel will probably try to steal it anyway. A pair of work gloves follows, the kind with leather palms that remind me of Papa Mark's hands.

"Back again?" Jake calls from behind the counter, that amused half-smile already in place.

"Of course. Your hens were the best deal I've made since I landed in this country," I say, hefting the basket onto the counter with a grunt. "They're laying steady, and they've got more personality than Emmanuel, which is saying something."

Jake snorts. "That goat of yours has personality to spare."

"Personality," I echo, "and criminal intent."

He chuckles as I pluck a blue halter with brass fittings off the wall and add it to the pile. "Cookie deserves to feel pretty," I explain.

"Pageant cow, huh?" Jake grins.

"She's earned it. Patient, steady, and she gives me milk even when Emmanuel is screaming at the fence line. That deserves a prize."

Jake starts ringing things up. "Need bedding too?"

"Feed, bedding, grit... oh, and I wanted to ask about ducks." I lean on the counter, lowering my voice like it's a secret. "I'm not sure if I'm ready yet, but I like the idea of fresh eggs and maybe a pond out back."

"Ducks are a whole different ballgame," Jake says. "Messier than chickens, but worth it if you've got the patience. If you're serious, I'll keep an ear out—sometimes folks around here sell off a flock when they can't keep up."

"Patience is debatable," I mutter. "But I'll add it to the list."

He bags everything neatly, and I'm sliding cash across the counter when the door slams open behind me. A gust of cold air rushes in, accompanied by the heavy thud of boots.

"Patrick, I'm telling you, he's on the damn roof," a deep voice growls into a phone.

I whip around. Adam. His expression is thunder, his ball cap low over his brow, and his attention locked on the phone pressed to his ear.

"Yeah, the barn roof," he says into the receiver. "No, I'm not joking. Get Brandon to grab the rope. I'll get her."

Her.

Me.

He shoves the phone into his pocket, eyes locking on mine. For a second, everything freezes. His gaze is fire and flint, and the sheer force of it makes my breath catch.

Then he jerks his head toward the door. "Your goat's on the roof."

The entire feed store goes quiet.

Jake sputters. "The roof?"

"Yes," Adam says flatly. "Chewing on something that doesn't belong to him."

My stomach plummets. "Emmanuel," I whisper.

Adam nods once, grim as a funeral. "Come on."

I snatch the bagged supplies from the counter, slap down the rest of my cash, and bolt after him. Heat rises in my chest, part panic, part fury. Of course Emmanuel picked today to attempt murder by altitude.

Adam's truck is parked half-crooked outside. He doesn't wait for me, just stalks toward it. I follow in my Jeep, tires spitting gravel as we race back to the farm. My grip on the wheel is white-knuckled; my pulse is hammering.

By the time I pull into the drive, chaos is already in full swing.

Patrick has his hands on his hips, looking like he wants to lecture the goat. Eli is doubled over, laughing so hard he can't breathe. Brandon is rattling an empty feed bucket like a goat whisperer who's lost all credibility.

And there, on the barn roof, is Emmanuel. Chewing my gardening hat.

I slam my Jeep door and stomp toward the barn. "Emmanuel, *espèce de petit démon*! That is not food! Get down this second!"

He stares at me with zero remorse and keeps chewing.

Laughter ripples behind me. Then a cough. Then all four brothers try not to collapse.

"If you wanted to donate your hat to the goats, you could've just tossed it in the paddock," Adam calls.

"You're awfully chatty for someone not helping," I snap.

"Oh, I'm helping. Moral support."

I march around the barn and grab the ladder. Hauling it over, I mutter curses in French and English. Emmanuel watches me from his perch, still chewing like he's earned a snack break.

"Get down. That hat was expensive!"

He turns and climbs higher.

"Don't you turn your back on me! I will not take you to the vet if you fall and break something. You'll just have to live on crutches. Forever."

"I'm sorry," Adam says behind me, voice low. "What exactly do you think you're doing?"

"Going up to get my goat off the roof."

"You're not climbing that ladder."

"Oh, I am."

His eyes darken. "No. You're not."

"What do you suggest? I politely ask him to levitate down?"

"I'll get him," Adam mutters. "Brandon, hold the ladder. Patrick, rope. Eli—stop recording."

"I wasn't!" Eli lies, shoving his phone into his pocket.

Adam climbs before I can argue, rope coiled in one hand. I cross my arms and try not to look impressed. Or worried.

He approaches Emmanuel slowly. "Hey, buddy. Let's not be stupid, okay?" Emmanuel tilts his head, sizing him up.

"Good," Adam murmurs. "Just a little closer—"

The goat launches. Everyone screams. Emmanuel lands in the dirt, shakes himself off like nothing happened, and struts back to the paddock.

I slap a hand to my chest, heart pounding. "Are you kidding me?! He could've broken every bone in his body!"

Adam looks down from the ladder, eyes blazing. "You mean to tell me he could've jumped down this whole time?"

Emmanuel lets out a victorious bleat.

Adam jumps down from the last rung, dust kicking up around his boots. He's still scowling, but the flush on his neck hasn't faded. For a long moment we just stare at each other, the world shrinking down to the space between us. Emmanuel bleats from the paddock like he's mocking us, but neither of us looks away.

Then his gaze dips to my mouth—quick, unguarded—and back up again. The shift burns through me hotter than the August sun, leaving me raw and unsettled.

I step back before I do something reckless. "I should check on Emmanuel," I say, my voice thinner than I want it to be.

His jaw tightens. "Do that."

The air between us hums with everything unsaid. I turn toward the paddock, refusing to let him see how my hands tremble—not from fear, but from something far more dangerous. Because for one impossible second, I wanted him to stay.

Chapter Fourteen
Adam

I watch that damn goat strut into the paddock like he just won the county fair and laugh under my breath—until I see her slip in after him.

The humor dies.

When my boots hit the ground, I'm already storming toward her, chest tight, ready to let loose. She could've gotten hurt. Really hurt. And for what? A hat? A goat with a death wish? But before I can open my mouth, she collides with me like a five-foot-nothing missile.

"Thank you so much," she mumbles against my chest. Her voice trembles, and that shakes me harder than anything Emmanuel just pulled. "I don't know what I would've done if he'd gotten hurt."

Her fingers twist in my sleeve like she needs an anchor. She's still shaking—I can feel it, right through the flour-dusted flannel of my shirt. Touch isn't rare on a ranch, but this... this is something else. My hands hover at her waist, useless, like I don't know what to do with them.

"I'm not worried about the goat," I manage, my voice rough. "I'm worried about you. You could've broken your damn neck climbing up there. Then where would you be? Dead."

The words come out sharper than I mean, but fear rides shotgun with my anger. I grip her shoulders, holding her still, like maybe I can undo the sight of her marching toward that ladder like it was nothing. "If that idiot animal ever pulls a stunt like that again, you come get me. Or Brandon. Or Eli. Hell, call the sheriff—you like doing that. But you do not go up there yourself. Do you hear me?"

Her head snaps up, blue eyes flashing fire.

"Let the men handle the dangerous work," I finish, the wrong words slipping out before I can bite them back. "You keep your lady feet on the ground."

Her glare could flatten a bull. Then she shoves me. Hard. My back slams into the barn wall. The old boards creak and dust drifts down from the rafters, stinging my eyes. Emmanuel bleats from the paddock like he's laughing.

"*Tu te prends pour qui*?!" she snaps, French cutting through the air like a whip. I don't need to understand it to know she just cursed me out.

She jabs a finger into my chest. Then another. "You think you can boss me around just because you don't like how I do things?"

I catch her wrist on the third jab before she breaks a rib. Her pulse hammers against my fingers. I should let go, but I don't. Not yet.

"I'm trying to keep you alive," I growl, the words scraping out louder than I mean.

"I don't need your help," she spits back, chin tilted high, fire rolling off her in waves.

The barn hums with it—our voices, the echo of Emmanuel stamping his hooves, Duke barking from somewhere beyond the fence. Dust motes swirl in the slant of sunlight cutting through a crack in the wall. The whole damn farm feels like it's holding its breath.

I should stop. Let her go. Walk away. But I don't. Her wrist is small in my hand, warm, strong, trembling just slightly. And she's so close. Too close. Her hair brushes my jaw, smelling like cinnamon and hay. Her lips part like she's ready to strike—or to do something far more reckless.

"I've taken care of myself for a long time, *mon cher*," she hisses, her accent sharp as steel. "I don't need some self-righteous cowboy telling me what I can and can't do."

"You think this is about control?" I lean closer, my breath grazing her temple. "It's about not wanting to see you laid out in a hospital bed. Or worse."

Her breath stutters. For one bare flicker, her eyes soften. Not rage. Not defiance. Fear. Not of me but of how close she came to losing something. Maybe someone. My grip on her wrist loosens, but she doesn't pull away. Not right away.

The space between us hums. Charged. Dangerous. My gaze dips—just for a second—to her mouth, before I drag it back up. I shouldn't. God knows I shouldn't.

And then—

"Wooooo-hoooo!" Eli's voice splits the moment in two. He rounds the corner, grinning like a jackass, his phone raised.

Christiane jerks back like she's been burned. She wraps her arms around herself, the fire in her eyes shuttering to steel. "Merci beaucoup pour ton aide," she mutters, colder now, not looking at me. Then softer, broken around the edges: "Thank you... for helping. I have to go."

She spins and all but runs to the house, the screen door banging shut behind her.

I round on Eli. "You are such a prick."

"What'd I do?" he says, all innocence.

I don't answer, just shoulder past him. A second later, Eli yelps. I turn back just in time to see him stumbling, clutching his ass. Emmanuel stands smug at his side, looking like he's been waiting all day for the moment. Maybe that goat's smarter than I thought.

🐾🐾🐾

Back at the house, I barely step through the door before Brandon whistles from the couch. Patrick glances up from his coffee with one eyebrow raised.

"You okay, Romeo?" he drawls.

"Don't start," I mutter, hanging my hat.

Brandon stretches out, arms wide like a king on his throne. "So... you and Christiane, huh?"

"It's not like that," I say, dropping into my recliner.

Patrick smirks. "Could've fooled us. Sparks fly every time you're in the same damn zip code."

"More like we've been at each other's throats since day one."

"Exactly," Brandon says, grinning. "The tension's doing half the work."

I glare. "I don't look moody."

"You do," Patrick says. "Like a bull about to charge. It's entertaining."

Their laughter fills the room, easy and loud, but I can't shake the memory of her. I feel her pulse under my fingers. The way she looked at me, like she couldn't decide whether to slap me or kiss me.

"Look," I say finally, voice low. "She's stubborn. Frustrating. Always got something to say. And yeah... maybe I don't hate seeing her around."

Brandon's brows shoot up. "But that doesn't mean anything."

Patrick shakes his head, smirking. "You're in trouble, Adam."

They keep ribbing each other, arguing about dinner, but I lean back in my chair and stare out the window. Her curtains are drawn. The house is quiet. And all I can think about is what would've happened if she had climbed that ladder. If she'd fallen. If I hadn't been there. For the first time in years, I'm not sure what scares me more—losing the land... or losing her.

Chapter Fifteen

Christiane

The screen door slams behind me, rattling in its frame as I storm into the kitchen. My boots strike the floor with sharp, angry thuds. Coat off. Keys tossed. The silence that greets me feels heavier than Adam's words, heavier than the look in his eyes when he said I could've been killed.

"Insufferable. Arrogant. Stubborn," I mutter in French and English, pacing a line across the kitchen tiles. Every word he threw at me still stings, and yet underneath the sting is something worse—the way his anger had sounded like fear. Fear for me.

I press a hand to my chest as if I can scrub it away. I can't.

The air feels tight. My body buzzes with restless energy, and the only cure I know is work. Baking. Precision and patience. Muscle memory. Something I can control.

Flour. Sugar. Salt. I measure with trembling hands, the sound of the scoop scraping the bowl steadier than my breathing. Yeast blooms in warm milk. I stir, watching bubbles rise like tiny promises, fragile but alive.

My sleeves are rolled up before I realize I'm still in my boots. Doesn't matter. I throw myself into the rhythm: press, fold, turn. The dough resists, elastic and stubborn. So do I.

Maman's voice floats through memory. *Soft hands, ma chérie. Let the dough breathe.*

I blink hard, but the ache in my throat doesn't fade. Folding butter into dough should not feel like a lifeline, and yet here I am, repeating the pattern over and over. Roll. Fold. Chill. Roll. Fold. Chill.

The sun fades outside, shadows stretching long across the yard. By the time I shape the dough into long triangles, the kitchen is lit gold from the last spill of daylight. Croissants curl into crescents beneath my fingers, delicate armor against the storm inside me.

When they bake, the kitchen warms, the air filling with the scent of butter and memories. I brush them with egg wash slowly and deliberately, watching the shine catch the dim light like glass.

When they're done, I pull the tray out. The layers are crisp, flaky, and tender. I tear one open, and steam curls up into my face. One bite, and the knot in my chest loosens—not gone but softened.

Still, I can't bear the thought of eating them at my empty kitchen table. Not tonight.

I fetch the picnic basket from the pantry and line it with a towel. Croissants go in first. Jam. Brie. A thermos of coffee. If I pretend it's a meal for more than one, maybe I won't feel so alone.

Outside, dusk is pooling violet at the edges of the fields. The barn loft draws my gaze, quiet and high, promising a vantage point where no one—especially Adam—can see me fall apart.

Basket in hand, I cross the yard. The goats follow, curious shadows at my heels. Emmanuel bleats, louder than the rest, and makes a daring lunge for the basket.

"Non," I warn, jerking it out of reach. "You are not auditioning for *Cirque du Chèvre*. Go chew on a stick. A respectable stick. Not couture pastry."

He rears up like he's thinking about it anyway, but I march past him toward the barn.

The metal ladder clatters as I prop it against the loft. Emmanuel circles below, bleating, plotting. I climb carefully, balancing the basket, ignoring the way my stomach flips at the height.

The loft greets me with a smell of hay and dust, sweet and dry. The boards creak under my boots as I settle near a beam and lower the basket beside me. Sunlight filters in slants through the gaps, catching dust motes that swirl like tiny dancers in the air.

Below, the goats shuffle and snort. Cookie huffs near the fence line, indifferent to the chaos. For a moment, it almost feels like a sense of peace.

I tear a croissant, spread it with jam, and take a bite. It melts on my tongue—flaky, soft, sweet. My throat tightens anyway.

Adam's voice sneaks back in. Laid out in a hospital bed. Or worse.

Not anger. Not control. Fear.

I close my eyes, back pressed to the beam, and let the soundscape wash over me. Crickets are tuning their evening song. The low moo of cattle far off. Even Emmanuel is pacing like a restless child.

For a moment, I can almost believe I belong here. That I'm not a foreigner, not an intruder. That maybe *Maman* and Papa Mark would be proud of me for standing my ground—even if it's harder than I let on.

Rattle.

My eyes snap open.

Another rattle.

I crawl to the edge of the loft and look down just in time to see Emmanuel headbutt the metal ladder. It rocks once, then again, then crashes to the ground in a tangle of silver.

"Emmanuel!" My voice cracks.

He stares up at me, beard twitching like he's laughing.

I grip the edge of the loft and glare down. "Put it back!" I hiss. "You knocked it down, you fix it. That's how this works."

He bleats louder, pawing at the fallen ladder. I throw my hands in the air. "Fantastic. My fate is in the hooves of a goat. Brilliant."

Panic pricks at the edges of my chest. I dig through the basket, napkins, and brie and jam tumbling over. No phone. Of course. I left it in the kitchen.

I press my palms to my eyes and groan. "This is why I bake for people and not goats."

The bleating continues. So does the pacing. Until—

A bark cuts through the dusk. Low, sharp, urgent. Duke.

My heart leaps. "Duke!" I scramble to the edge, leaning over. His golden fur flashes as he trots into the yard, tail wagging. "Go get Patrick, Duke! Go get Patrick!"

He barks again, bounding off toward the fence line. Relief rushes through me, shaky and fast. Maybe luck hasn't completely abandoned me.

Bootsteps crunch against the gravel a few minutes later. I grip the edge tighter, whispering, "Please be Patrick. Please be Patrick. Hell, I'd even take Eli. Just not—"

A shadow rounds the barn. Broad shoulders. A familiar cap pulled low. My stomach sinks.

Of course.

Adam.

Of *fucking* course.

"Christiane."

The ladder is gone, Emmanuel is prancing victory laps below, and I'm stranded in the loft with nothing but a basket of croissants and the man who makes me want to scream and... something else I can't admit.

And the worst part is... Adam Williams is the only way down.

Chapter Sixteen

Adam

A clatter rings out from the barn, followed by Christiane's voice, sharp enough to slice the air.

"Emmanuel! Put it back! Duke—go get Patrick! Go!"

Duke bolts across the pasture like his tail's on fire. I mutter a curse, drop my rake, and jog after him. Trouble's never far when that goat's involved.

By the time I reach the barn, Duke's panting at the door. Inside, Christiane is stranded in the loft, arms crossed tight, flour smudged on her cheek, braid unraveling. A wicker basket is clutched to her side like a lifeline.

"Please be Patrick. Please be Patrick," she mutters. Then her eyes land on me. "Of course. Of fucking course."

I tip my cap. "Evening to you too, sweetheart."

"Where's Patrick?"

"Not here. You've got me instead." I prop the rake against the wall. "Sorry to disappoint."

She groans. "God must really hate me."

"Or he likes a good joke." My gaze drops to the ladder in two busted pieces. "That thing's not gone, it's dead."

She gestures fiercely. "Then fix it. Unless you'd prefer I sleep up here."

I breathe in dust, hay, and the faint curl of butter from her basket. "Hang tight."

"I'm very literally doing that," she snaps. "Try not to take a scenic route."

I drag square bales into a stack beneath the loft. The thumps echo, dust rising with every shove. Duke sits by the door like a foreman on break.

Christiane leans on a beam, unimpressed. "If this is your version of rescuing, I'm not impressed."

"Good thing I'm not trying to impress you. What's in the basket, Red Riding Hood?"

"Food."

"That's specific."

Her chin tips up. "Croissants."

My stomach growls. Figures. "You bake those?"

"What do you think?"

"I think you brought snacks to a crisis."

"Unlike some people, I come prepared."

I shake my head, climb the stack, catch a beam, and haul myself up. Dust blooms. She scowls, clutching the basket closer.

"Took you long enough."

"You're welcome," I shoot back, brushing straw off my jeans.

The loft feels smaller than it looked from the ground. Her pulse ticks in her throat; butter and coffee hang in the air. I should step back. I don't.

Then Emmanuel trots in, smug as a king.

"Oh, perfect," Christiane sighs. "The villain arrives."

The goat noses my bale tower, finds a twine knot, and yanks. The whole stack slumps and collapses in a dusty thud. Emmanuel bleats in triumph, then wanders off to harass a glove.

Christiane exhales, long and dramatic. "Well, now we're both stuck."

We stand shoulder to shoulder, staring at the wreck. The barn creaks warm around us, crickets tuning up outside. For a moment, I don't mind being trapped. That should bother me.

"You could thank me," I say.

"For what?"

"For climbing up here instead of letting you sleep with the croissants."

She hugs the basket tighter. "I still might."

She kneels, opens the lid, and the smell of butter rolls out. She breaks one in half and hands me a piece. Our fingers brush, and heat shoots through me.

"You're dangerous," I murmur.

"Because I can bake?"

"Because I might forgive you anything if you hand me food like that."

Her laugh slips free, startled and real. She takes a bite, then passes me a chipped mug from the basket. Coffee. Hot, dark, perfect. We drink from it in turns, knees nearly touching, the loft closing around us.

"I told Duke to get Patrick," she says after a moment.

"I know."

"You are not Patrick."

"Unfortunately for both of us."

Her jaw works. "Why do you do that? Turn everything into jokes."

"Because if I don't, I'll say something worse."

"Like what?"

"Like I ran when I heard you," I say, low. "And I don't run for people."

Her gaze catches mine. The barn holds its breath. I reach, slowly, and tuck a strand of hair behind her ear. She doesn't pull away.

We lean—almost. The air hums, charged.

"Adam," she whispers.

My name in her mouth feels like yes, maybe, and don't you dare all at once.

Then Emmanuel slams a horn into the hay below, bleating triumph. She laughs under her breath, and the sound brushes my mouth.

"Do not rescue me again," she says.

"Stop needing it," I answer.

Silence stretches. She smirks. "I don't hate you as much as I want to."

"Same."

The light fades to blue. She shivers, stubborn about it. I peel off my hoodie and drop it in her lap. She glares, then pulls it on. It swallows her hands, smells like cedar and hay and me. That should not thrill me as much as it does.

She tucks her knees up, looking at the dark gap in the boards. "What do we do now?"

"Wait for the brothers. Or yell. Brandon always wanders by."

"And if he doesn't?"

"Then we wait till morning."

She wrinkles her nose. "I refuse to sleep in a hayloft with you."

"That's a shame," I say, and she smacks my arm.

More quiet. More dangerous. I tip my head until my temple rests against her hair. She lets it.

"You were right earlier," she murmurs.

I grin. "Say that again."

She elbows me. "You were right about one thing. I don't hate you as much as I want to."

"Same," I say again, softer this time.

We don't kiss. We don't climb down. We just sit there—croissants, coffee, goat mischief, and all—until the barn folds around us and the night feels very far away.

Chapter Seventeen

Christiane

The barn feels too small with Adam in it. Too hot, too loud, too much. His shoulders fill the space, his voice soaks the air, and his eyes—God help me—his eyes pin me in place.

I fold my arms tight and snap, "Don't look at me like that."

He leans one shoulder against the beam, maddeningly calm. "Like what?"

"Like you think I needed rescuing."

His mouth quirks. "Funny. You prayed for Patrick." He tips his cap. "You got me."

I mutter something sharp and very French under my breath, hugging the basket closer. Emmanuel crashes around below like he's in on the joke. The stupid goat's probably smiling.

Adam smirks anyway, like I amuse him even when I'm furious. "You're welcome, sweetheart."

My jaw tightens. "Stop calling me that."

"Why? Because you like it?" He shifts closer, straw crunching under his boots.

"I do not."

His grin deepens. Infuriating. "Prove it."

"I don't have to prove anything to you."

He laughs, low and rough, and I can't help the shiver that goes down my spine. "That's what I thought."

The air between us feels heavy, and his nearness makes every inhale thick. I turn away, desperate for distance. "This is ridiculous. We need a plan."

"You already had one," he says. "Climb without thinking it through. Worked great until it didn't."

I whirl on him. "Oh, so now I don't think things through?"

He pushes off the beam, stepping closer. "What would you call that?"

"I'd call it bad luck. Which, let's be honest, seems to happen every time you're around." His gaze drops too fast, too sharply, to where my shirt has slipped off one shoulder.

The barn is cool, but suddenly my skin feels hot, prickled under his stare. I shift like I mean to stand, to pace, to escape, but the floor creaks treacherously beneath me. His hands are on my waist before I can protest, steady, calloused, warm. I freeze. The world narrows to his grip, firm and unyielding, and the way his breath brushes my temple. My heart kicks hard against my ribs.

"Let go," I whisper, though even I hear the lie in it. His grip tightens.

"You sure?" I should be, but I'm not.

"No," slips out before I can stop it, and Adam doesn't hesitate. His mouth crashes into mine, rough and searching, stealing the air straight out of my chest. My back hits the wall of the loft, hay scratching my sweater. I'm lost in the heat of his body, energizing me like nothing else ever has. The kiss is wild, consuming, impossible to fight. His hand cradles the back of my neck like I'm breakable, like he can't risk letting me go. I fist his shirt, yanking him closer, needing more.

When he breaks away, barely, his eyes blaze with fire and hesitation both. It guts me, that flicker of doubt. He's giving me an out. He's letting me choose. I chose wrong. I grab his shirt and pull him back to me. He groans into my mouth, the sound reverberating through me, and lifts me as though I weigh nothing.

He lays me down in the hay with surprising care, his big body covering mine. His hands slide beneath my sweater, dragging over my skin slowly, reverently, devastatingly.

"You're driving me insane," he mutters, voice gravel-deep, his breath hot against my ear.

"Good," I whisper back, tugging him down. My fingers dig into the firm muscles of his back, earned from years of manual labor. Our clothes vanish, tossed aside with urgency until there's nothing but his heat and my hunger.

When he mouths over my skin, reverent and greedy all at once, I'm wrecked. His lips and teeth trace a path of fire and ice, leaving me gasping and arching, offering everything, demanding more. His teeth graze sensitive flesh, soothed immediately with soft kisses, and I cry out, unable to hold it back, my voice echoing in the empty barn.

"You sure?" he asks again, softer this time, like he needs me to say it twice. I nod, breathless.

"I've never been more sure." And then he's inside me—slow, deep, perfect. The stretch of him is almost too much, and I cling, gasping, as he groans into my neck, his body trembling. I wrap my legs around his waist, pulling him closer, deeper.

"Christiane," he groans, burying his face in my neck, his voice a ragged whisper. "You feel so damn good."

He starts to move, and I match his rhythm, meeting each thrust with one of my own. It's not rushed—it's consuming. Desperate. Our bodies speak the words we can't, the hay scratching my back, the barn creaking around us. Somewhere below, Emmanuel bleats in protest, but I barely register it. All I can feel is Adam: his body moving against mine, his breath mingling with my own.

The pressure builds again—tighter, hotter—until I'm teetering on the edge. He reaches between us, thumb circling my clit with maddening precision, his touch sending lightning through my veins. I shatter quickly and with an intensity that rips through my body. I clench around him, and he groans, hips slowing as he comes with a sound that makes my toes curl. We collapse onto the loft floor, breath ragged, limbs covered in hay.

Rolling over, Adam brushes sweaty hair from my cheek with a tenderness that undoes me more than his roughness ever could. "Are you okay?" he asks quietly.

I nod but words fail. I didn't expect this. I didn't expect tenderness. He chuckles softly, low and tired, kissing my shoulder without thinking. It's intimate in a way that terrifies me more than anything we just did. The barn creaks. Emmanuel snorts below. Duke huffs like he's standing guard. Reality seeps back in.

I grab my shirt from the hay, tugging it over me with a sudden, sharp motion. The fabric drags rough across my skin, and with it comes a wave of cold that has nothing to do with the night air. Beside me, Adam buttons his jeans, each movement stiff, deliberate, like he's building armor one piece at a time. He drags his hoodie back over his head, shadowing his face, and for a moment, he looks like a stranger again.

"This was..." I start, but the words catch in my throat, tangled in the weight of everything unsaid.

"Yeah," he says, his voice equally raw, a mirror to my own turmoil. "It was."

We fall quiet, but it's not the easy, comfortable silence of two people at peace. It's charged, jagged, alive—an unfinished thing that pulses between us, heavier than the hayloft air.

I tuck myself into one end of the loft, wrapping the blanket tighter around my shoulders, seeking solace in the warmth that can't quite reach the chill in my bones.

He stays at the other end, broad shoulders hunched in the dim, his head tipped back like he's fighting demons I'll never see. The sight of him—so close, yet unreachable—twists something deep inside me. Between us, the silence grows, louder than shouting, of things left unsaid, of desires and fears that dance just out of reach.

And I know this isn't over. It's barely begun. The tension between us is a taut string pulled to breaking, and I don't know whether I want it to snap or hold forever.

His eyes meet mine, storm-dark, and I see it all—the struggle, the need, the fear—and I wonder if he feels it too. The relentless tide that threatens to drown us both.

And yet some traitorous part of me wants to drown with him.

Chapter Eighteen

Adam

The silence in the loft is jagged, sharp as broken glass. Christiane's curled in the far corner, blanket clutched around her shoulders like armor. I sit opposite, hoodie pulled tight, every breath full of hay dust and regret. The ghost of her lips still burns on mine, but she won't even look my way.

Then Eli's voice rips through the night.

"Adam!"

I flinch, the sound snapping the fragile thread between us. Christiane's head jerks up, eyes wide, but she doesn't speak.

I drag in a breath, force my voice out. "We're up here! Bring our ladder—this one's done for."

Below, Emmanuel bleats like the smug bastard he is, stomping once for emphasis.

Christiane wraps her arms closer around her waist. When her voice comes, it cuts me deeper than any curse.

"Why?" Her gaze pins mine, hard and searching. "Why have you been so nasty to me?"

The words hit like a fist. I want to joke, to deflect, but I can't. Not now. Not after everything.

I swallow hard. "Because I didn't want you here."

Her breath catches. Her chin tips up, proud even as her eyes shine. "What?"

"You don't belong here, Christiane. Not on this land. Not in my world." My voice scrapes raw, every word jagged with truth. "I've spent twenty years trying to put my family's name back where it should've been. My grandfather lost everything because of my father—his gambling, his drinking. I've fought for every acre back. And your property... it was supposed to be the last piece. The finish line. Then you showed up, and I didn't know what the hell to do."

The confession hangs heavy in the rafters. She doesn't cry. Doesn't yell. She just stands, slow and deliberate, brushing hay from her legs with movements so careful they might shatter her if she falters.

"I thought if I was cruel enough, you'd leave," I say more softly. "That you'd sell. Walk away. But you didn't."

Her voice is a whisper, exhausted and empty. "No. I didn't."

"And now," I admit, hating myself, "I don't know how to let you go."

Her eyes glint in the dim light, unreadable. For one impossible second, her fingers brush mine, featherlight. Hope stirs like a fool in my chest.

"You could've just told me," she says, quiet but sharp. "Instead, you tore me down every chance you got. You still could choose honesty now."

The faintest smile tugs at her lips, brittle as glass. I want to believe it's a beginning. But guilt chews through me until I choke on it.

"You still need to go," I whisper.

Her hand drops. The flicker in her eyes snuffs out. She steps back like my words shoved her.

"Eli!" I bellow, my throat raw. "Bring the ladder. Hurry it up."

From below, Emmanuel answers with a bleat that sounds far too much like disapproval.

Christiane's voice slips out, so quiet I almost miss it.

"I wish I'd never moved here."

The words cut deeper than a blade. And I just stand there, useless, choking on all the things I'll never say.

The barn door groans open wider, spilling lamplight across the dirt floor. Eli's silhouette fills the space, the ladder balanced on his shoulder as if it weighs nothing.

"Well, well, well." His voice is full of laughter. "What'd you two do now? Loft date gone wrong?"

"Shut up," I growl, heat crawling up my neck.

He props the ladder against the loft, still smirking. "Just saying—takes a special kind of talent to get yourselves trapped *together*. At night. With snacks." His gaze flicks to Christiane's basket. "Croissants, no less. Damn, brother, you sure know how to pick your crisis snacks."

Christiane doesn't rise to the bait. She just gathers her basket and climbs down without a word, every line of her body screaming distance.

Eli whistles low. "Cold shoulder. Rough night, huh?"

I descend more slowly, boots thudding on the rungs. My brother steps back, arms folded, eyebrows high. "Want me to grab a couple of sleeping bags? Y'all looked cozy."

I shoot him a look sharp enough to cut. "Drop it, Eli."

"Fine, fine." He lifts his hands, mock innocent. "Just saying, if Emmanuel hadn't busted that ladder, I'd have bet money you'd still be up there."

I don't answer. Because he's right.

That night should've been a beginning. Instead, it was the breaking point.

Christiane's words linger, echoing in my chest like a bell I can't un-ring. *I wish I'd never moved here.* They haunt me long after Eli's ladder rattles against the loft and we climb down in silence.

The next morning, I tell myself maybe she didn't mean it. Maybe it was just anger, humiliation, the goat's chaos, and my own damn mouth piling on until she snapped. Maybe if I give her a night to cool off, things will ease.

So I give her time. A day. Then another. At first, I think she just needs a few more. That space will fix it, like it usually does. That if I keep my distance, she'll come around.

But space doesn't fix it. Space kills it.

Before I realize it, days have bled into weeks. Weeks into a month.

I see her everywhere—at the feed store, at the market, on her porch hanging laundry, Emmanuel tugging a rope at her side like a dog. But she doesn't look at me anymore. And when she does, it's like I'm part of the scenery. A fence post. A tree line. Nothing more.

At first, I think it'll fade. That she'll cool off. Forgive in that quiet way she has. But it doesn't.

She sharpens.

Her words cut shorter. Colder. The French lilt that used to slip in when she was flustered is gone. Now her voice is clipped, clean edges that don't leave room for me.

At the feed store, I hold the door without thinking. She breezes past without a glance, without a word.

At the market, I buy a jar of jam just to have an excuse to see her. She takes my money like it's a chore. "Enjoy," she says, flat as stone. Like I'm no one.

And it stings more than I'll ever admit. The worst part? I start chasing it.

I needle her on purpose, her fence, her goat, her bread prices—because when she snaps back, at least she *looks* at me. Sparks in her eyes, venom in her voice. It's better than the void.

But it's different now. She doesn't fight me like I'm worth fighting. She dismisses me, like she's burning the bridge behind her.

And I can't stand it.

I lie awake nights, hating myself for needing her anger just to feel her near. Replaying the loft until it's raw.

I tell myself I don't care. That she's just a woman who bought the wrong land at the wrong time.

But every time she cuts me dead in public, every time her gaze slides past me like I'm nothing, something in me twists so hard it feels like it might break.

I should let her go.

Instead, I keep finding excuses to stand too close. To say the one thing that'll draw her eyes.

Because as much as I hate her silence, I hate myself more for needing her to break it.

I wake with a start, sunlight cutting across the room like a blade. Something's wrong. I feel it before my feet even hit the floor.

No smell of pastry drifting across the fields. No faint glow in her kitchen window. Just cold. Empty.

I shove on jeans and boots, the wrongness thickening in my chest like smoke. Out of habit, I check the drive before heading out. Her Jeep's gone. My pulse jumps.

Maybe she went to the diner. She's been slipping over early most mornings since the renovations started, watching progress with a mug of coffee in hand, like it steadies her. The thought is enough to get me moving.

Gravel spits under my tires as I swing onto the road. The closer I get to town, the harder my grip tightens on the wheel. I round the corner, expecting to see Paul's truck out front, tools spread across the sidewalk, the buzz of saws or the thud of hammers.

But the diner sits silent. Windows dark. A *closed* sign hanging crooked in the glass. No Paul. No Jeep. Just plywood stacked by the door and the kind of stillness that sinks straight into my gut.

I slam the truck into gear and head straight for Paul's place.

He steps onto the porch before I'm even out of the cab, wiping his hands on a rag, surprise flashing across his face.

"Where is she?" I demand, too sharp, too fast.

Paul frowns. "She's gone, Adam."

The words hit like a hammer to the chest. I grip the porch rail like it's the only thing keeping me upright. "Gone where?"

His expression shifts, unreadable. "Back to France."

The air leaves my lungs. My vision tunnels. "Why?"

"She didn't say. Just that she needed to go."

The rag dangles uselessly from his hand, but all I see is the space she's left behind. My jaw clenches so hard it hurts.

I told her to leave. I pushed and pushed—and she finally listened.

And now she's gone.

Gone, and I don't know if she'll ever come back.

Gone, and it's my damn fault.

Chapter Nineteen
Christiane

Adam's words ring in my ears every time I blink. You don't belong here. He meant the land—he always means the land—but the sentence spread like weeds, rooting under my ribs, in my sleep, in every silence.

I told myself to ignore him. To stand taller. To bake until the whole house smelled like butter and belonging. To hammer fence boards until splinters looked like proof. I told myself I didn't care.

But I did. And I'm tired. Bone tired. I can't keep doing this.

So I pack.

My hands move fast, shaky but sure—shirts shoved into a duffel, jeans rolled until the seams strain, socks tossed without caring if they match. Not neat. Not careful. Just escape.

Maman's cookbook goes last, wrapped in a tea towel that still smells faintly of cinnamon. I scribble feed charts for Daisy, Dandie, Debbie, and Paisley—four hens, I whisper out loud, as if naming them will keep me tethered. Emmanuel butts my hip, insistent. "Shh," I murmur into his ridiculous little beard. "It's only for a while."

The Jeep rumbles in the drive, loud enough that Duke lifts his head in question before settling again. I drive with both hands clenched on the wheel, the road unspooling in streaks of gravel and gray light. The town blurs past—feed store closed, diner dark, fields folded in sleep. I don't let myself stop.

The airport is a fog of lines, announcements, and the kind of waiting that makes time both endless and too short. Step by step, until New York shrinks into a patchwork quilt far below me. Hours later, Paris unfurls silver beneath the wing. I press my forehead to the glass and watch rooftops gather like a tide.

By dusk, the village lane greets me—lavender lining the road, nothing changed. And yet everything in me has.

At the family cemetery, the grass behind the orchard dips into a hollow where the soil is soft. That's where the stones are—simple, pale, carved by a neighbor who owed Papa Mark a favor. I used to count my steps from the kitchen door to the lavender row. Forty-nine when I was little. Forty-three when I grew. Now I don't count. My body knows.

I kneel between them—*Maman* on the left, Papa Mark on the right—and brush away leaves. The air smells of thyme and damp stone. Down the hill, a tractor coughs awake.

"I finally have a farm," I tell them, and the laugh that escapes is thin. "Smaller, messier, but mine. There's a goat who thinks he's king and four hens who trail after me like children. Cookie, my cow, got a new blue halter. I miss you."

I set down a bouquet of rosemary and lavender, pressing my palms to the earth. *Maman* always said soil remembers hands. I close my eyes and try to feel remembered.

"I thought it could be—" Love. Home. Family. "—something." The words snag in my throat. "But it was never mine to keep."

Papa Mark's voice rises from memory: *La terre, ça s'apprivoise. Il faut du temps.* Land takes time.

"I tried," I whisper. "I tried so hard."

The wind stirs the lavender. Not an answer, but enough to stand on. I rise because standing is what I know how to do.

❦ ❦ ❦

"You have exactly three minutes to feel sorry for yourself," Margot declares, carving into cheesecake like she's on trial counsel. "Then we switch to strategy."

"It's cheesecake," I say. The slice is Parisian-clean—no heavy crust, just delicate crumb and raspberry coulis pooling like a mended heart.

"It's leverage." She slides half onto my plate. "Sugar first, then logic."

Le Comptoir glows the same as always—brass, lamplight, the hum of conversation, our waiter saving us the best table while pretending he despises us. We've closed this place countless times—birthdays, breakups, that infamous foie gras stunt. But tonight, the edges blur, as if I'm walking through memory instead of life.

"You've been sulking for two weeks," she says.

"I'm not sulking."

"You left half your wine." She gestures, scandalized. "You. I should call a doctor."

A thin laugh escapes. "I'm fine."

"You're not," she says, softer, serious now. "You didn't choose to come back. You let him push you here."

"He said I didn't belong."

Margot rolls her eyes. "Yes, the poet. And did you—alone—turn an empty house into a working farm in under three months?"

"Yes."

"Wrangle a goat named after the apocalypse? Convince a cow to wear jewelry?"

"Her halter is tasteful."

"Exactly. You didn't inherit it. You built it."

I stare at the raspberry stain on my plate. "It felt like it could have been... everything. But I misread him."

"You wanted a future with someone who can't see past his ghosts." She slices neatly. "That's not on you."

The door chimes. A breeze carries rain and laughter. A man in a navy blazer leans on our table, smile rehearsed. "*Bonsoir*. I couldn't help overhearing—"

"Can't you see I'm busy?" I ask sweetly, not looking up.

Margot smirks. "She bites."

He retreats. I pop a whole raspberry. "I forgot how good it feels to be terrible with you."

"We perfected it in primary school. Remember when *Madame* Rousseau put baking powder in crepes and you called it criminal?"

"I was nine."

"And impossible." She grins. "We were always going to be this."

We. The word unclenches something in my chest.

"So," she says briskly. "Strategy. Two lives. Which one is yours?"

"I don't know."

"Try this: which one is not?" She points her fork like a compass. "If you stay, is it because you want France—or because you're hiding from him?"

"I'm not hiding."

"Need me to make a spreadsheet?"

"Please don't."

We eat in silence earned by years of telling truths without flinching. When the plates are crumbs and pink smears, she nudges my ankle. "When are you going back?"

I watch the couple outside arguing with deep intimacy. Love and fury wear the same shoes. "I can't answer that."

"You can," she says, squeezing my hand once. "And you will."

When we leave, our waiter tucks two madeleines into the check. We slip them into our bags like sinners, practiced and unrepentant.

❧ ❧ ❧

The Paris air is cool, rain-tanged, alive with traffic and laughter. To me, it's just noise.

Margot loops her arm through mine. "Come home with me. Balcony, wine, pigeons."

"I can't. Not tonight."

Her eyes narrow. "Back to that sterile hotel room?"

"It's quiet there."

She sighs, cupping my cheek. "Fine. But don't drown in that quiet. I've seen you build a life out of flour and fire. Don't let him steal that."

The lump in my throat makes speech impossible. I kiss her cheek, whisper, "Merci," and step away.

The walk back is longer than it should be. Every glowing café window feels like a reminder of what I left behind.

Lavender oil blooms in the hotel bathroom, steam ghosting the mirror. The tub is deep enough to swallow me. I sink, let the water lap my chin, stare at the ceiling. Paris roars outside—scooters, applause, bass thudding from a club—but here it's only me, breath and water.

I dunk my head, come up gasping, hair slicked to my skull. For a heartbeat, I feel undone—and better for it. But when I close my eyes, I see the loft. His mouth. The half-inch we didn't leave between us. The memories assault me until the water cools and I drag myself out of the tub. I pull on the robe, pad to the desk. The city blinks through sheer curtains. I drag the hotel notepad close and scrawl two columns.

New York
- I earned that farm.
- Emmanuel (menace, walnut brain, lion heart).

- Cookie's blue halter.
- Four hens, four opinions.
- Early mornings, dirt under my nails.
- The patisserie dream.
- A second chance.
- Home?

France

- Familiar.
- Margot.
- The orchard. The family plot.
- Safe.
- No Adam.

The last line looks petty. I strike it. Then write it again, smaller. Truth, even ugly, deserves a chair.

I add one word to New York: **Courage.** I cross it out. Then write it again.

My bag lies open on the chair, *Maman's* cookbook on top like a heartbeat. I touch the frayed tea towel to steady myself.

A knock jolts me. Firm, rattling the glass.

Another. "Christiane."

That voice. Low, rough, too familiar.

"Open the door."

Every muscle locks. My feet are rooted to the carpet.

"Damn it, Christiane." A scrape—his palm against the wood. "Open the door and talk to me."

A thousand exits flash—bolt it, call the desk, hide. None real. Behind the fear, something sharp threads through my ribs.

Hope. Treacherous. Alive.

I stand. One step. Another. The brass of the handle is cold under my damp fingers.

I press my ear to the door. He breathes like a man who ran too many stairs. For the first time in so long, I don't feel alone.

The latch clicks. The door opens an inch. His eyes are darker than I remember.

"Bonsoir," I manage, because I can't say what's under it yet.

"Hi," he rasps, gaze flicking from my robe back to my face. "Can we talk?"

I don't move. I don't let him in.

But I don't close the door either.

Chapter Twenty

Adam

I've counted every single hour since she left.

Two weeks. Fourteen days. Three hundred and thirty-six hours.

And for the first ten of those, I didn't know where she was.

Didn't know if she was safe. If she was eating. If she was thinking about me the way I thought about her—with equal parts longing and guilt, both cutting me wide open.

Mason came through like he always does. We've been friends since college, and there's no one better at tracking down someone who doesn't want to be found. When he handed me the file—pages of notes, photocopies, photos, fragments of her life I'd never bothered to ask about—something inside me cracked open.

She wasn't just the woman with a loud goat and a stubborn streak.

She had roots. Losses. A whole damn story I'd never cared enough to learn.

I don't open it right away.

I sit in the truck, parked under the buzzing fluorescent light of a gas station, engine off, night pressing in heavy. The file lies on the passenger seat as if it weighs fifty pounds. My hand hovers over it once, twice, before I finally flip the cover.

Christiane Devereaux.

Her name, printed neat across the tab, feels foreign. Too formal. Too cold.

It doesn't belong to the woman who curses in French at a goat or leaves flour streaks on her cheek without noticing. It doesn't belong to the woman I kissed like I was drowning, then pushed away with words I can never take back.

The first page is a school photo. She can't be more than eight years old. Cardigan buttoned to the throat, posture stiff, mouth pressed into a line while the rest of the class smiles widely. Her eyes, God her eyes are wary. Like she already knows the world can turn cruel without warning.

There's a note scrawled on the side that states it was taken not long after her father's death.

The next is her and her *maman* at a spring festival. Wildflowers are braided into Christiane's hair. Her mother is in a sundress, arm wrapped around her girl. Both caught mid-laugh, like someone shouted a joke right before the shutter. That photo feels like sunlight—too bright for me to be holding with my calloused hands.

The one after nearly undoes me.

Her *maman* and Papa Mark on their wedding day. Simple, small, just them under a flowering tree. Christiane stands beside them, maybe ten years old, clutching a bouquet too big for her hands, grinning widely. She looks like she finally belongs.

And then the farm.

She's twelve, maybe thirteen, with mud streaking her calves, her hair wild from a braid, a basket of eggs hugged tightly to her chest. Another on a crate, reaching into rafters. Another at sixteen, leaning against a fence with Papa Mark, both of them laughing, dust curling in the air. She looks free. Like the land is hers and she's its.

Then graves.

Her *maman's* first. Christiane is eighteen, standing beside the stone, eyes swollen but dry, Papa Mark's hand heavy on her shoulder. Then another, later—two stones side by side.

She's alone now. Coat buttoned high. Hands jammed into her pockets. Shoulders hunched like she's trying to make herself smaller.

She isn't crying.

She's hollowed out.

My chest aches like someone drove a spike straight through it.

I don't realize I've reached for my wallet until I'm sliding one of the photos inside—Christiane barefoot in a sunlit field, crate of eggs in her arms, smiling like the world hadn't betrayed her yet. I tuck it behind the photo of my mom. I don't know why. Just that it feels right. Like I need to carry her with me this time. Because I can't let her carry everything alone anymore.

I book the first red-eye out of JFK. I pack a bag with more panic than purpose.

The flight feels endless. Five, six, seven hours in the air. I tell myself I'll sleep. I don't. I stare out the window, watching the black ocean turn gray then silver. My reflection in the glass looks older than I remember—drawn, hollow-eyed, like a man who's been running from his own damn shadow for too long.

A family sits a few rows ahead, two kids squabbling over a stuffed bear while their mother divides snacks. The father rubs his wife's shoulder, quietly and easily. I can't stop watching them; I can't stop thinking about how badly I've screwed up something I didn't even let myself admit I wanted.

Paris spills out under the wing in a sprawl of rooftops and stone, a tide of silver in the morning light. I press my forehead to the glass, hating that I notice the way it smells different when we land—damp stone, diesel, coffee sharp in the air. Her world. Not mine. And I'm intruding again.

The rental car is small, underpowered, but I shove my bag in the trunk and drive anyway. Six hours through farmland and stone villages. Lavender fields flash past, and I hate that I catalog it. Hate that I know what she'd say about the way the light hits, the way the air tastes cleaner here.

Every mile closer tightens the thread in my chest until I swear bone might splinter.

It's late when I pull into the hotel's gravel lot. The facade is quiet, windows dark. My pulse drums so hard I feel it in my throat.

The lobby is dimly lit, illuminated by a single desk lamp. The clerk barely glances up, unimpressed by the unshaven

American who is dripping fatigue across his counter. I don't blame him. I slide a bill across the wood, my voice rough.

"Christiane Devereaux. Please."

He sighs like I'm ruining his night but finally scribbles a number on scrap paper. 212.

I take the stairs, two at a time. My footsteps echo, breath ragged, hands shaking by the time I hit her door.

I knock. Once. Twice. Louder until my knuckles sting. Until my forehead presses against the frame.

Fear crawls through me. What if she's not here? What if another man answers? What if she opens it just to tell me to get the hell out?

I knock harder, voice breaking. "Christiane."

Nothing.

"Damn it, Christiane." My palm flattens against the wood. My throat scrapes raw. "Open the door. Talk to me."

The latch clicks. The door creaks open an inch.

And there she is.

Christiane.

Her robe is belted tight at her waist. Hair pulled back. Barefaced. Beautiful. But guarded. She doesn't move aside. Just blocks the doorway with her body, holding her ground.

"Adam." Her voice is soft. Not broken, but not whole either.

My chest lurches. I rake a hand through my hair. "I—" The word breaks in my throat. I force it out again. "I never should've acted like I did. I knew it wasn't right. But I thought..." My voice cracks. "I thought you'd be safer away from me."

Her expression doesn't shift.

"I wanted you to trust me," I go on, words raw, tumbling out fast now. "But I didn't trust you. That's on me. I was so busy protecting what I thought mattered that I couldn't see what actually did."

Silence stretches. Heavy. Crushing.

"You deserved better." My voice lowers. "And I made you feel like you didn't matter when you were the only thing that did."

Her gaze doesn't waver. My chest tightens with every second she stays silent.

"I told you to leave. But I didn't mean it. I didn't want you to go." I take a step closer. She doesn't move back. Doesn't move forward either. Just... holds.

"I've spent twenty years chasing land, legacy, redemption. Thought if I got it all back, I'd feel whole again. But it's nothing without you." I lift my hand, palm open. No demand. Just hope. "You were the last thing I thought I needed. But you're the thing I need most."

She doesn't take my hand.

But she doesn't close the door either.

And for the first time in weeks—

I let myself hope.

Chapter Twenty-One
Christiane

Adam's words hang between us, heavy as the silence. His hand is there—open, steady, waiting—but I can't bring myself to take it.

I don't close the door either.

For a long, breathless moment, we just stand like that. Him in the hall, me in the doorway, everything between us balanced on a thread I'm too afraid to touch.

The scent of him fills the narrow space—jet fuel, leather, sweat clinging to skin that hasn't seen sleep in too long. His shoulders slump like he carried the ocean here with him, but his eyes... his eyes are still fierce, still fixed on me like I'm the only thing holding him upright.

My palm flexes on the door. I could slam it now, shut him out before he worms his way any deeper. For one dizzy second, I almost do. But then his voice cracks, rough and low, and the sound nails me in place.

Finally, I let the door swing wider. Not an invitation. Not forgiveness. Just... space.

"Come in," I whisper.

He steps inside, and the air shifts. The hotel room feels smaller and hotter, as if it's struggling to accommodate both of us. He doesn't sit. Doesn't pace. Just stands there looking at me like he's memorizing my face, like it might vanish if he blinks.

"You don't get it, do you?" His voice is rough, scraped raw. His hands curl tight at his sides like he's afraid of what they might do. "I never wanted you to leave. I told you to go because I was a coward. Because I thought if I pushed hard enough, I could protect everything I'd been chasing—legacy, land, pride. But none of it mattered. Not compared to you."

The apology lands, sharp and late. Anger flares through me, but under it something smaller stirs. Hope, treacherous and alive.

"I don't know what to believe anymore." I wrap my arms around myself, trying to hold the pieces in place. "You pushed me away when I needed you most. You told me to leave. Do you even remember that? Because I do. Every night."

His jaw tightens. "I was wrong. God, I was wrong. But you can't just walk away from me. From us."

"Us?" I laugh, sharp and bitter. "You don't get to say that word. Not after what you did." I turn from him, pacing toward the window, my reflection fractured in the glass. "You think you can just show up, say you're sorry, and fix it? Do you know how many times I replayed that night? Do you know how small you made me feel?"

Silence stretches, thick enough to choke. His boots scuff against the carpet.

Then he's there, closer than I realized, his hand hovering near my arm but not quite touching. His voice drops, rough and reverent. "I can't undo it. But let me show you. Let me prove I can be better."

My throat tightens. I should shove him away. Instead, I whisper, "Show me?"

The space between us collapses. His lips crash into mine, and I meet him with equal fury. It isn't gentle. It's desperate, hungry, years of walls shattering in an instant. His hands fumble at the knot of my robe, pausing as if he's afraid that if he pulls it loose, I'll vanish. For a heartbeat, I almost clutch it tighter. Almost say no. But then his thumb drags over my lip, trembling but steadying me all at once, and I let the fabric fall open.

His gaze sweeps down, hungry and reverent, lingering on every inch like he's memorizing me for the rest of his life. When his shirt comes off under my hands, I see the faint scars that map his chest—white lines, sunburnt patches. Proof of years I never asked him about. Proof of how human he really is.

Adam parts my robe like he is opening the greatest gift, his eyes trailing over me, and I swear I can feel them on my skin. Ducking down, he wraps his mouth around a nipple, teeth scraping and teasing, and I can't stop the noises that fall from my mouth. Rough hands slide down to part my legs, and my body arches into his as he settles between my thighs. His cock is hot and harrowing as it slides between my folds, and I shudder with each bump against my clit. I am so turned on that there is no resistance when the head of his cock lines up with my entrance, pushing inside with one smooth thrust.

The sheets rasp against my back, thin hotel cotton, nothing like the scratch of hay or the softness of quilts back home. Paris hums outside the window—horns, scooters, laughter spilling up from the street—but in here it's only us. His breath, my gasps, the rhythmic thud of the headboard knocking against plaster.

Our groans mingle together, our lips inches apart, as Adam starts to move. The stretch is a pleasant burn as I adjust to his width again, his thrust picking up speed and intensity. "Fuck me harder, please." The words slip out before I can stop them, but Adam's body answers my plea, and my nails leave crescent thank-yous in his skin.

My legs start to shake, and I know that I am close. Opening my eyes, I meet Adam's, and I know when I finally go over that cliff, he is going to be there with me. The fact that he is here and inside me tips me over the edge, and I scream out his name as my body clamps tight around him and he fills me, and I let go, every piece of me giving way.

My thighs still quake, the tremors rolling through me long after the peak fades. His chest is damp under my cheek, heartbeat hammering wild against my ear. For a few stolen breaths, I let myself sink there, let myself believe this is safety instead of the most dangerous place I could ever rest.

But then the silence creeps in, louder than the city outside, and the ache in my chest returns sharp as ever. He shifts, turning toward me. His hand brushes my arm, tentative, almost shy. "I don't deserve this," he says quietly. "I don't deserve you. But I want to try."

I close my eyes. Tears slip free, hot against my temples. My voice comes out as a whisper, fragile and uncertain. "Then don't make me regret it."

His hand lingers, warm and steady. For the first time in weeks, I let myself breathe.

Chapter Twenty-Two
Adam

The room is quiet except for our breathing. She's sprawled across the sheets, skin still flushed, hair tangled, lips swollen from my kiss. Beautiful. Wrecked. Mine.

My hand rests on her stomach, palm spread wide, grounding me in the reality that she's here, with me. She doesn't push me away. She just turns her face toward me, eyes half-lidded, mouth parted like she wants to speak but doesn't.

"Christiane," I murmur, brushing a soft kiss over her shoulder. "I don't deserve this. You."

Her gaze flicks to mine, sharp but searching. "Then why?" she whispers. "Why now?"

I press my forehead to hers, my voice low, steady, even though my chest feels like it might split open. "Because I was a fool. I thought the land was all I had left of who I was. My grandfather poured his life into it. When my father lost it, I swore I'd fix it, even if it killed me. I thought if I got it back, I'd matter again."

Her fingers trail along my jaw, slow and deliberate. "And now?"

"Now I know none of it means a damn thing without you," I admit. The words scrape raw out of my throat, but they feel truer than anything I've ever said. "Land doesn't keep me warm at night. It doesn't laugh when the goat knocks over a bucket or sing to chickens when no one's listening. You do."

Her lips tremble. She shakes her head, a breathless laugh escaping her. "You're saying all the things I told myself I'd never hear from you."

"I should've said them sooner," I whisper, kissing her knuckles, lingering there. "But I'm saying them now."

She studies me, eyes shimmering in the half-light. Then her hand slides lower, over my chest, across my stomach. Her touch is soft but sure, and my body reacts instantly, tightening under her palm.

"And what if I don't believe you?" she asks, her voice thin but steady.

"Then I'll spend the rest of my life proving it."

Her eyes flick away, her throat working. "You already spent months proving the opposite," she whispers. "Do you have any idea how hard it was to crawl out of that? To stitch myself back together when you tore me down?"

Guilt slices through me. My hand finds her face, thumb brushing her cheek. "I do now. And I'll never forgive myself for it."

Something shifts in her gaze then, a flicker of hope cutting through all the hurt. She kisses me, and it's different this time. Slower. Hungrier. Like she's testing the weight of my words with her mouth. My hand moves to her hip, fingers sliding over the familiar curve of her body, and she arches into me, her breath catching.

The storm sparks to life again, hotter, stronger, pulling us under.

"I want to take my time with you," I murmur against her lips, my voice rough, shaking with everything I'm holding back.

Her throat works as she swallows. For a heartbeat, she looks uncertain, but then she whispers, low and firm, "Then do it."

The words nearly undo me.

My hands move slowly, reverently, skimming her collarbone, down to the swell of her breast. Goosebumps rise under my touch, her breath hitching with every inch I claim.

She lets me. She trusts me. And it wrecks me all over again.

I lower my mouth to her skin, kissing the hollow beneath her ear, tasting salt and warmth. She shivers, and her nails graze my back, pulling me closer. My hands wander her body, mapping her like I've never touched her before.

Her gaze is heavy, hot, as her fingertips trail over my chest, down my stomach, tracing old scars. She looks at me like she's memorizing, and it undoes me more than anything. I catch her wrists gently, stilling her.

"Not yet," I whisper.

She looks up at me, wide-eyed, and nods without a word.

I kneel between her legs, sliding my palms up her thighs, parting them just enough to fit myself between. The air between us hums, heavy, sparking.

I kiss her stomach, slow and open-mouthed, lingering there. She shudders, fingers curling in my hair, pulling me closer. Her body trembles under my hands, and I press another kiss higher, then lower, savoring every inch of her.

"I want to learn you," I murmur against her skin, looking up at her.

Her breath stutters. She nods, whispering, "Then learn me."

And I do. Slowly. Thoroughly.

Every kiss is deliberate. Every touch is worship. Her breath grows ragged, her body arching, and when she gasps my name, it's not a plea, it's a command. I give until she comes apart in my arms, her nails digging into my shoulders, her body quaking against me.

When I finally move over her, sliding into her slowly and deeply, she meets me with equal fire. This time there's no desperation, no frantic clawing at what we're afraid to lose. Just rhythm. Just heat. Just the truth of us.

Her eyes lock on mine, fierce and unblinking, and I know I'll never be the same.

We move together until the world burns away. Until every wall I've built, every sharp word I've spoken, crumbles to dust. Until there's only us—messy, raw, unguarded.

When it's over, I stay inside her, our foreheads pressed together, our breaths mingling in the dark.

"I'll never let you go again," I whisper.

Her hand cups my jaw, her thumb brushing my mouth like she's weighing the truth of it. "Don't just promise, Adam," she murmurs, voice trembling. "Compromise with me. Tell me you'll fight for both of us this time. Not just the land. Not just your pride. Us."

I close my eyes, the weight of her words cutting through me like scripture. "I will. I swear it."

And for the first time in my life, I mean it.

Chapter Twenty-Three

Christiane

The heat between us finally fades, leaving only the steady rise and fall of our breathing in the quiet aftermath. My head rests on Adam's chest, the soft thump of his heartbeat grounding me, as if that sound alone could hold me together. His hand traces lazy circles across my shoulder, slow and absent, and for a moment, I let myself melt into it—into him.

For a fragile heartbeat, I let myself believe.

Then he ruins it.

"When do you want to head back to Willow Glen?"

The spell shatters like glass.

My body stiffens, pulse spiking, and I push up on one elbow, staring down at him in disbelief. "When," I demand, "did I ever say I was going back?"

Adam blinks, clearly caught off guard. His brows pinch together, confusion and something heavier flickering across his face. "Well, I just figured—"

"You figured?" I cut in, sharp, my voice shaking as a scoff escapes before I can stop it. "You just assumed I'd pack up and follow you back like some lost puppy?"

His jaw tightens, muscles ticking. "That's not what I meant."

"Then what did you mean?" The words come out low and dangerous, but beneath the bite is hurt. Hurt that runs deeper than I want to admit.

Adam sits up, dragging a hand through his hair. The sheet falls to his waist, and suddenly, he looks less like the man who kissed me senseless an hour ago and more like the one who's broken me before. "Christiane, your place is in Willow Glen. Your farm, your animals—it's your home."

I stand, clutching the sheet around me, and cross the room. The tile is cold beneath my bare feet, grounding me in a way his words can't. My fingers curl around the edge of the dresser like it might hold me steady.

"Right now, my place is here," I say, turning back to face him. "I promised Margot I'd help her at Le Petit Trésor for three more weeks. I gave my word, and I don't break my promises."

He exhales sharply, frustration radiating off him. "You don't owe them anything. You gave them more than enough already."

"It's not about what I owe them," I snap, heat rising in my chest. "It's about me. She's my best friend in the world. And I'm not just going to walk away because you think you get to decide where I belong."

His hands curl into fists at his sides, blue eyes dark and stormy. "I'm not used to people arguing with me about this kind of thing."

A sharp laugh escapes me. "Yeah. I can tell."

His jaw clenches. "Christiane—"

"No, Adam." My voice cuts like glass as I tug the sheet tighter around myself. "You're used to getting your way. You're accustomed to making decisions and having every-one else follow suit. But that's not me. You don't get to dictate my life."

He stares at me for a long moment before muttering, almost to himself, "Stubborn as hell."

Despite the tension, my lips twitch into a smirk. "Right back at you."

I turn away, facing the window where the early morning light spills across the floor in soft gold. Maybe I do want to go back eventually. Perhaps I miss the farm more than I want to admit—the way the sun caught on the barn roof, the sound of Emmanuel's hooves clattering against the porch, the quiet rhythm of my fields.

But I need to go back on my own terms. Not because he asked. Not because he assumed. I won't lose myself again.

❦

The next few weeks at *Le Petit Trésor* pass in a blur of flour-dusted mornings and late-night sugar rushes. The air is always thick with the scent of butter, yeast, and strong coffee. The kind of smells that cling to your clothes and your hair, so much so that even when I collapse into bed at night, I still breathe it in.

It should have been exhausting. Instead, I find a strange comfort in the rhythm of it all—the kneading, the proofing, the careful spin of the espresso machine. Each step is measured, precise, something I can control when the rest of my life feels uncertain.

However, there has been one unexpected constant in my days.

Adam.

Every morning, without fail, he strolls into the patisserie like he owns the place. And every single morning, he attempts to speak French.

Badly.

The first time, I thought he was just being polite. But after the second, third, and fourth attempts, it became clear—he was trying. He was trying to understand my world and meet me in it. And damn it, it's ridiculous and endearing all at once.

Today, he approaches the counter with his usual swagger, flashing me that smirk that used to infuriate me but now makes my stomach flip. "*Un café avec*...uh...*fromage?*"

I blink, biting back laughter as Pierre, one of the older bakers, furrows his brow. "*Fromage?*"

Adam nods, proud of himself. "*Oui.*"

A few minutes later, Pierre returns with a tiny espresso and a wedge of brie neatly arranged on the saucer beside it.

Adam stares at it as if it has betrayed him. "Uh...this isn't what I meant."

Pierre shrugs. "You asked for coffee with cheese. Voilà."

The entire kitchen bursts into laughter, mine loudest of all. Adam glares at me, but there's no real heat in it. "You think this is funny?"

I nod, tears stinging my eyes. "You asked for it, *mon cher*."

Something in his expression softens at the endearment, his mouth tipping into a reluctant grin. "Fine. Laugh it up."

And it doesn't stop there. The next day, he tries ordering a croissant with honey—except instead of "*miel*," he says "*merde*." The kitchen erupts into chaos, Margot nearly chokes on her tea, and Pierre threatens to serve him something far worse than cheese.

By the end of the week, Julien, the dishwasher, keeps a tally of Adam's linguistic disasters on a chalkboard by the register. Every failure is written with a flourish, and every time Adam sees it, he grumbles but smiles anyway, swearing he'll hold a whole conversation in French before I leave.

I have my doubts.

But through it all, something shifts between us. We fall into an easy rhythm—sharing stolen moments over steaming cups of coffee, lingering at the end of the day when the patisserie grows quiet. He helps me close up, rolling his sleeves and washing dishes without being asked. Sometimes he kneads dough with more strength than finesse, flour streaking his forearms, looking at me like he'd do this every day if I asked.

And he never once pushes me to leave.

Instead, he keeps showing up. Proving in a thousand little ways that he's here for me.

And damn it, it's working.

The patisserie is still now, the kind of stillness that only comes once the world outside stops watching. Outside, the streets of Paris are empty, the lamps glowing softly in the fog. Inside, it's just us.

I rest my hand on the counter's edge and glance at him. His shirt's untucked, his hair a mess from running his fingers through it all night. His eyes find mine and hold, steady and searching, like I'm the decision he's been waiting for all along.

He doesn't speak. Just watches.

I cross the room slowly, my heart pounding harder with each step. I stop in front of him. "You never push."

"No," he says quietly. "But I never stop hoping."

The words break something in me. I don't answer. I just rise onto my toes and kiss him—slow, sure, steady.

His hands find my waist, sliding up my back, tentative, like he's waiting for me to change my mind. I don't. I press closer, deepening the kiss, and something shifts in the air around us. It goes tight, electric, humming with everything we haven't said.

We don't rush.

His mouth moves over mine with reverence, as if he's learning me all over again. My hands slip beneath his shirt, fingers dragging across warm skin, and I feel his breath stutter against my lips. He lifts me gently—no bravado, no urgency—and settles me onto the edge of the prep table. The metal is cool beneath my thighs. He's warm everywhere else.

We move like we've done this before, but now we know what it means.

This time isn't about proving anything. It's about choosing each other. Right now. Right here. Not as a promise. Not as a compromise.

Just as something real.

Chapter Twenty-Four
Adam

The morning in Paris feels nothing like back home. There's a crispness in the air that sharpens the edges of everything—the leaves, the light, even the sounds. As we stroll through the Bois de Boulogne, the world feels slower and softer. Like the city wants to keep its secrets a little longer. A warm bag of croissants swings between us, and beside me, Christiane is smiling.

Really smiling.

She tears off a piece of pastry and hums as she pops it into her mouth, eyes fluttering shut for a second like it's the best thing she's tasted in weeks. Maybe it is. Perhaps it's just that here, in her city—her language, her rhythm, her sky—she looks like she belongs.

Like she's lighter. Like the weight she's carried has loosened just a little.

I've never seen her like this. And it hits me harder than I thought it would.

"Still can't believe you ordered *un croissant avec jambon* this morning," she says, elbowing me with that teasing grin that makes it impossible not to smile back.

I groan, rubbing a hand over my face. "I thought I was asking for butter, not ham. How the hell was I supposed to know?"

She laughs, bright and unfiltered. "Because I told you yesterday that butter is *beurre.* And yet here we are—you eating a ham croissant at eight in the morning."

"I didn't eat it," I protest. "I gave it to that guy at the next table."

She grins wider. "That guy thought you were flirting with him."

I nearly choke on my coffee. "Wait, what?"

"Oh yes," Christiane says, far too pleased. "When you handed it to him and said *bon appétit,* he winked at you."

I groan again. "Fantastic. I'm out here accidentally flirting with Frenchmen and humiliating myself."

Her laughter is the kind of sound I want to bottle. Pure joy. It cuts through the months of tension and uncertainty like sunlight breaking through storm clouds.

We settle onto a bench near the lake, where the water glimmers beneath the early sun and ducks glide by like little boats with no destination. Around us, Parisians pass by with dogs and newspapers, their pace slow and their smiles knowing. The kind of quiet confidence this city breeds in its people.

She looks out across the water, and something in her profile catches me—nostalgia maybe, or some flicker of longing I haven't yet earned the right to ask about. The breeze tousles her hair, and she leans into me just slightly, the warmth of her shoulder grounding me in a way nothing else has in weeks.

"You look different here," I say after a moment.

She glances at me, her brow raised. "Different how?"

"Lighter. Like your skin fits better."

She looks away, blinking. "My mom used to take me to the markets here, and Papa Mark would take me to festivals near the river. I used to think I'd stay in France forever."

"What changed?"

She smiles, but it doesn't quite reach her eyes. "Grief makes everything feel smaller. Sometimes the only way to breathe again is to leave."

I nod, letting her words settle and become part of the quiet between us.

My phone buzzes in my pocket, shattering the moment. I pull it out and see Patrick's name flashing across the screen with a video message.

"Looks like Patrick needs something." I tap the screen.

Patrick's face fills the video, lit by the glow of a barn light. His voice is low, tired, the kind of cadence that says he hasn't had dinner yet and would rather be in bed. "Hey, Adam. Just thought you'd like to know Emmanuel is at it again. First, we found him on top of the chicken coop—don't ask me how. Then he got into the feed shed and helped himself to dessert. After that, he headbutted two garden gnomes into the pond. And now he's standing on the hood of my truck, looking very pleased with himself. Any chance Christiane wants to come back and handle her goat before he starts running night patrol?"

The camera shifts, catching Emmanuel silhouetted against the headlights, bleating like a warlord who's con- quered new territory. Eli yells something off-screen, and

Brandon groans like a man already over it. Patrick just sighs. "Anyway. Thought you'd want to know. Night, brother."

Christiane snorts beside me. "Honestly, this sounds like a regular Tuesday for Emmanuel."

I shake my head. "You refused to sell him after he ate your favorite hat. At this point, I think you have Stockholm Syndrome."

She shrugs, unfazed. "Maybe. But he's cute."

"He's Satan," I mutter. "A tiny, black, four-legged demon."

"He has personality," she argues, nudging me again.

I can't stop watching her, not even when the video ends with Patrick trying—and failing—to coax Emmanuel off the hood. The goat just stands there like royalty, surveying his kingdom.

We sit there for a while longer, sipping coffee, watching the ducks, and sharing the last croissant. Her head rests against my shoulder, and for the first time in what feels like forever, it feels like maybe we've stopped running.

Then Christiane speaks, her voice barely above a whisper. "I've been thinking..."

I turn toward her.

"Maybe it's time to go home."

The breath I didn't realize I was holding slips out. "You mean it?"

She nods, a small, tentative smile curving her lips. "Yeah. I think I'm ready."

I slide my hand into hers, squeezing gently. "Together?"

"Together," she says, and I believe her.

We don't pack right away.

Instead we give ourselves one last night in the city. Dinner at a tiny bistro near Montmartre, where the candles burn low and the waiter winks when Christiane orders in quick, flawless French. Afterward, we walk along the Seine, the water catching every gold ripple of the streetlamps. She leans into me, her hand slipping into mine, and for the first time in years, I feel the kind of peace you don't have to earn.

When we reach her hotel room, she doesn't hesitate. She takes my hand and pulls me inside.

It's different from before—slower, softer. Not desperate or angry or fueled by months of sharp words. This is about choosing. About staying. About pressing her back to the sheets and kissing her like we have all the time in the world.

I worship her with patience, with reverence, until she breaks apart under me, clutching my shoulders and gasping my name. When I finally slide into her, we move together in unhurried rhythm, learning each other all over again. Her eyes lock on mine, fierce and unflinching, and in that moment, I know we're both choosing this.

When it's over, we stay tangled, her cheek pressed to my chest, my hand stroking slow circles along her back. She whispers, "Thank you for not rushing."

I kiss her hair. "I don't want to rush anything with you ever again."

The next morning, we pack. Christiane stands at the window of her hotel for a long while before we leave, her gaze stretched across the rooftops. She doesn't speak, but I see it—the goodbye she's saying in silence.

On the plane, she curls against me and sleeps, her hand tangled in mine. I stare out the window at the shrinking lights of Paris, and for once, I don't feel the need to look back.

Hours blur into customs, baggage, and the long drive home.

The moment we cross back into Willow Glen, something shifts. The road narrows, the fields stretch long and gold around us, and the sound of sirens tears through the air.

My stomach drops.

Christiane grabs my arm. "Adam, what's happening?"

I don't answer. I drive faster, my heart pounding as we crest the last hill. Flashing red lights and a swirl of chaos greet us as we pull into the gravel drive.

I barely wait for the truck to stop before I'm out and running.

Eli is seated near the barn, a paramedic crouched beside him, his leg propped up on a folding chair.

"Eli!" Christiane calls, rushing to him.

He lifts a hand. "It's okay. Just a broken leg."

I stop short, breath burning in my chest. "What the hell happened?"

Eli winces. "Emmanuel. He got up on the barn roof again. I climbed up to get him down, and the little bastard head-butted me. I fell. Landed wrong."

"You should've waited for help," I snap.

Eli shrugs. "Didn't think I'd get tackled by a goat today."

Christiane looks ready to throttle him, but I see the fear still in her eyes. The tremble in her hands.

"You're not invincible," I say, touching Eli's shoulder. "Don't pretend you are."

"Yeah," Eli mutters, grimacing. "Noted."

The paramedics finish their work, and the sirens fade as the ambulance pulls away. The barn is intact, and the animals are safe, but something inside me is still off balance.

Christiane exhales beside me, her head lowering against my arm.

"Well," I say, still catching my breath. "We're dealing with a lot more than just a goat."

She lifts her head, eyes tired but smiling. "Maybe it's time we start building a better fence for Emmanuel."

I glance at her, relieved and wrecked and more in love than I was this morning. "Or maybe we just give him a castle. Seems like he's already crowned himself king."

Chapter Twenty- Five

Christiane

The quiet hum of the night surrounds us, the house settling into its own rhythm as we lie in bed, tangled in the warmth of the covers. The soft glow of the bedside lamp casts a faint halo on Adam's features, making him look almost too good to be true. His arm is slung lazily over my waist, his chest rising and falling in an oddly comforting rhythm.

I turn toward him, propping my head on my hand as I watch him. His expression softens when he looks at me—like he's still getting used to this, to us—and it sends a flutter through my chest.

"I've been thinking," I say softly, breaking the quiet. My voice feels small in the silence, but it's been circling my head all day.

"About what?" His voice is low, still thick with the quiet ease of the evening.

I let out a breath, glancing toward the window where the stars scatter like flour across dark velvet. "About the house. Paul took care of the urgent repairs months ago—the porch, the wiring, the roofline. Everything that kept it from falling in. But it still doesn't feel like home. Not yet. I keep telling myself I'll start the rest—paint, paper, the things that make it mine. But I've been putting it off. Maybe because if I start... it means admitting I'm staying for good."

Adam shifts, brushing my hair back with the flat of his hand. "You've carried enough weight just getting this far," he says softly. "I know how easy it is to put off the rest when the work feels endless."

I nod, my heart heavy but steady. "It's not just work. I want this place to be more than patched boards and faded wallpaper. I want it to feel like ours. A home."

He doesn't answer right away, just strokes his thumb over my arm like he's thinking it through. Then, "Let's finish it together. Paul got you this far, but now it's our turn. Paint, sanding, whatever it takes. I'll help."

I look up at him, meeting his gaze. His eyes are soft in the low light, and his smile is lazy but genuine. His words carry a quiet sincerity that settles deep inside me.

"You'd really help me?" I ask, my voice barely above a whisper.

He chuckles, pressing a kiss to the top of my head. "Of course. I'm not letting you do this alone. If you're making this place your home, I'll be right there with you every step of the way."

A smile tugs at my lips, my heart swelling with a mix of relief and hope. "Okay," I say, my voice soft but full of resolve. "Let's do it."

Adam's hand finds mine, fingers interlocking as he pulls me closer. His warmth is steady, grounding, and for the first time since I bought the Morrison place, I feel a flicker of excitement about what it could become.

This time, we'll make it a home. Together.

The following morning after a quick breakfast, we set up in the living room. The air already carries the sharp tang of fresh paint, mingling with the earthy scent of old wood. The peeling wallpaper is half scraped, revealing bare walls that show through like a canvas waiting for something new. I stand in the doorway for a moment, seeing potential instead of problems for the first time.

Adam glances up from the tray of rollers, a playful grin spreading across his face. "Ready to get your hands dirty?" he teases, holding a paintbrush like a weapon.

I smirk back. "You'd be surprised how much I enjoy getting my hands dirty."

He raises a brow, clearly amused. "I'll take your word for it." He presses the roller to the wall, the swish of paint a strangely satisfying sound. "I'll cover the big spaces. You can handle the edges."

"I think you just want to boss me around," I say, grabbing a smaller brush.

"Maybe," he admits, lips twitching. "But you're good at listening."

I roll my eyes, kneeling by the trim. "We both know who's really bossing who around here."

His low laugh makes the room feel warmer than it is.

We work in comfortable silence for a while, the room slowly transforming under our strokes. Each patch of color lifts the space, brighter and fresher, until I can almost see the home I've imagined.

"So," Adam says after a while, still focused on the wall, "the diner. What's your plan there? I know Paul's been working with you, but you haven't told me much beyond 'fresh floors and good coffee.'"

I smile, wiping a smudge of paint from my wrist. "I want it to feel like home. Not just for me, but for the people who come there. Warm, welcoming. A little French charm, a little down-home Americana. Somewhere people go not just to eat, but to belong."

He glances over, thoughtful. "You'll make it work."

Warmth spreads through me at the quiet conviction in his tone. "Thanks," I murmur, then tilt my head. "But enough about my plans. What about you? Twenty acres of cattle doesn't exactly run itself."

He wipes sweat from his brow with his forearm. "Patrick and Brandon are holding down the fort. They've got it. But I needed a break and," his eyes cut to me, softer now, "it's kind of nice being here with you."

My chest tightens, but in a good way. "I'm glad you're here."

"Me too," he says.

Before I can answer, a loud thud shakes the floor, followed by the metallic clang of something toppling.

We freeze.

"What was that?" I ask, spinning toward the doorway.

Emmanuel stands there, smug as a king. A tin of paint lies on its side, bright white pooling across the floor, streaking up his legs like boots.

I burst out laughing. "Emmanuel!" The scold dissolves into giggles I can't stop. The goat looks far too pleased with himself.

Adam, lips pressed tight in an effort not to laugh, finally loses it too. "Guess we found the one who's really getting his hands dirty."

The goat shakes his head, spraying flecks of paint across the room like a Jackson Pollock disaster.

I'm doubled over, wiping tears from my eyes. "Well, that's one way to add character to the place."

Adam tosses me a rag, still grinning. "Better get him cleaned up before he decides the walls need stripes."

I groan, tugging Emmanuel by the collar as he makes a grab for a fallen brush. "Come on, you little menace. Time for a bath."

Adam's laughter follows me out the back door, warm and easy, mixing with the sound of the goat's indignant bleats. For once, even chaos feels good.

When I glance back through the doorway, Adam is still painting, lips twitching like he's trying to hold in another laugh. The room smells like fresh beginnings. My chest swells with something I haven't felt in a long time—home.

This, I think, is what it feels like to stay.

Chapter Twenty-Six

Adam

The cattle move slowly in the afternoon heat, their lazy shuffling kicking up dust as I lead them toward the back pasture. The sun is high, pressing down like a weight, but I don't mind. Not today. A sense of peace out here settles into your bones when you've got a good woman to come home to. It still surprises me how much has changed in the past few months.

I find a spot near the creek, a patch of shade where the water runs clear and steady. Pulling a sandwich from my pack, I sit on the grass, stretching my legs out in front of me. The sound of the water and the rustling trees makes this a good place to think.

Lately, all my thoughts have been circling back to Christiane.

I hated her at first. Or, to be honest, I hated the situation. She bought the land that should've been mine, and I let that bitterness fester longer than I should have. But damn, if life didn't have a way of humbling a man. Because now, I can't imagine Willow Glen—hell, my life—without her in it.

She's changed everything.

I take a bite of my sandwich, chewing slowly as my mind drifts through the memories of the last few months. The long nights working on the house. The early mornings spent painting, repairing, rebuilding. The way she'd wrinkle her nose when something wasn't going right or flash that fierce grin when it finally did.

We spent hours pulling up warped floorboards in the living room one night. She insisted she could handle it. After an hour of wrestling with a crowbar and getting nowhere, she flopped on the couch, sweaty and annoyed.

"This house is testing me," she muttered, wiping her forehead with the back of her hand.

I sat beside her, setting the crowbar down with a grin. "Maybe it wants to see if you're serious about sticking around."

She turned her head, eyes tired but stubborn. "And what do you think?"

I didn't even hesitate. "I think you've already proven yourself."

And she had. The town had been cautious at first—small towns always are with newcomers—but she won them over slowly, steadily. Her work to get the diner set up helped. People were curious, dropping by to see the renovations, asking questions, offering advice. The French charm she carried with her, mixed with Southern staples she planned to serve, gave them a glimpse of what was coming. It all felt like something that already belonged here—familiar and new at the same time.Even Patrick and Brandon came around faster than I expected. And Eli? That kid would follow her into battle if she asked.

I smile to myself, remembering the day we re-tiled the kitchen. She'd gotten too confident with the mortar and smeared a glob across her cheek. I'd lost it—full-on belly laughing until she retaliated by smearing mortar across my jawline.

We ended up in a messy war, slinging mortar and laughter, Emmanuel hopping through the chaos like some four-legged gremlin. Tiny hoof prints tracked across the unfinished tile. We didn't even care.

That moment was the first time I let myself think: I want this to last.

I finish my sandwich and push to my feet, brushing crumbs from my jeans. The cattle still need to be moved, and the chores don't wait. But as I head back toward the pasture, one thing is clear. This land, this town, this life, it's not just mine anymore.

It's ours.

After a long day of work, I climb the steps to the house. The late afternoon sun casts long shadows, and a warm, sweet aroma greets me before I even reach the door. Christiane is baking.

Through the kitchen window, I catch a glimpse of her. She's spinning in place, dusted in flour, humming along to a soft French tune playing on the radio. Her voice floats through the air, light and carefree. She's radiant.

And at that moment, all I could think of was that I'd never felt more at home.

I open the door and step inside, taking in the smell of roasted chicken and potatoes and the faint hint of lavender from the open windows. The house is alive now. It breathes. It feels lived-in. It is loved.

She turns, catching sight of me, and her smile could bring a man to his knees. She crosses the room and kisses me without hesitation, and in that brief moment, everything feels quiet and sure.

"Adam!" she laughs as she pulls away, playful warning in her tone.

"Behave. My brothers are coming for dinner, and I won't have you looking like you've just been kissed senseless."

I grin, still close enough to steal another kiss if I wanted to. "Can't make any promises."

She shoos me toward the dining room, shaking her head with a smile. "Set the table, cowboy. I've got dinner under control."

I do as I'm told, grabbing plates and silverware and arranging everything just so. Every sound—the scrape of the chairs and the clink of the dishes—feels like a reminder. This isn't just a stop along the way. It's where I'm meant to be.

The doorbell rings just as I finish, and a few minutes later, Patrick and Brandon are inside, grinning like they own the place.

Patrick claps me on the shoulder. "Look at you. Domestic bliss looks good on you."

Brandon shakes his head. "And to think, we thought you'd die grumpy and alone."

"Thanks for the vote of confidence," I deadpan, smiling.

The evening moves in an easy rhythm. Food is passed around, stories are shared, and laughter spills into the corners of the room. The house is loud in the best kind of way; the kind that means it's full.

Even Eli emerges, still in a cast but moving more easily now, only leaning on his crutch when it suits him. He milks it for sympathy, but the doctor already told him he'd be out of it in another week or two. Tonight, his eyes are on the dessert tray.

"Eli!" I warn.

He grins, already stuffing one in his mouth. "What? It's tradition."

Christiane throws a dish towel at him, but she's laughing too.

And me? I sit back, taking it all in. The flicker of candlelight on the table, the warmth of Christiane beside me, the smell of sugar and butter still hanging in the air. This is what we've built. What we're still building.

A home. A life.

Together.

Chapter Twenty-Seven

Christiane

The dinner table glows in the soft light of the setting sun, and as I watch my new family gathered around it, I can't help but reflect on how far I've come. Just six months ago, after Papa Mark died, I felt utterly alone. Trapped in an empty hotel room with nothing but silence and grief for company. I was convinced I'd lost my home. That I'd lost myself.

But tonight, with the laughter bouncing off the walls, the aroma of roasted garlic hanging in the air, and a flaky croissant breaking apart between Eli's fingers, my chest aches like an old bruise. Faded. Familiar. But no longer ruling me.

Adam's brothers sit across from me. Brandon telling a wildly exaggerated story about a tractor malfunction, Patrick heckling every detail like it's his personal mission, and Adam just shaking his head with the kind of fond exasperation that tells me he's used to this. Eli's perched at the end, leg still in a cast, sneaking another croissant while the rest argue over who's doing the dishes.

"Eli," I warn gently, trying to hide my smile, "that's your third."

"It's broken leg immunity," he says, grinning without an ounce of shame. "Doctor's orders."

I laugh, and the sound surprises me—bright, real. It's been so long since I've felt joy that wasn't diluted by fear.

I carry the chicken and potatoes to the table, serving with trembling joy. Every dish I prepare now feels like a stitch mending something torn inside me. Every bite is a new memory laid over old wounds. The kitchen was my mother's sanctuary, Papa Mark's too, and now it's mine.

This... this is belonging.

When dinner slows and plates are pushed back with satisfied groans, I find myself leaning back in my chair, watching the others. Watching *him*. Adam is caught mid-laugh as Patrick mocks his serious face during "cow talk." A deep, quiet pride is etched into his features tonight, like he knows I've let something go. Maybe I'm not holding everything so tightly anymore.

Later, when the laughter has faded into soft murmurs and the house settles into the hush that only comes after good food and fuller hearts, I find myself in our shared room, curled beside Adam under the covers. The warmth of the evening lingers—not just in the lingering scent of roasted garlic and warm bread, but in the way his hand skims gently down my spine like he's tracing the rhythm of a song only he can hear.

I shift to look at him, propping my head on my hand. "Thank you for including me in your family," I whisper. "I never imagined I could feel so... whole again."

He smiles—slow, genuine—the kind that starts at his eyes and moves down to soften every edge of his face. "You're the most important part of my family, Chris. I've never been happier than when you're here."

The silence that follows is full of comfort, not tension. We don't need to say anything more. The way our bodies curve into each other beneath the sheets says it all.

I could fall asleep like this—warm and safe—but the ache to move and touch stirs under my skin. I slip out from under the covers, padding quietly into the kitchen. There's something grounding in the cleaning ritual. The quiet scrape of plates and the hush of warm water. I rinse the last dish, letting the suds swirl down the drain.

Behind me, the floorboards creak. I don't need to turn. I feel Adam's presence, familiar now, like a second heartbeat.

His hand slides gently across the small of my back, fingers splaying wide across the curve of my hip. His mouth brushes my ear, and his warm breath sends a tremor through me.

"You really did make tonight special," he murmurs.

I smile, still facing the sink. "And you always know exactly what to say."

His laugh is low and rough, his fingers tracing the seam of my arm. Goosebumps rise. "Sometimes I can't resist teasing you too."

I turn slowly, the plate still in my hands. His gaze is steady and intense. Like he's memorizing me again.

Then he takes the plate from my fingers, sets it carefully on the counter, and leans in, cradling my face as he kisses me. Slow. Sure. No urgency, just the warmth of familiarity and the thrill of choosing each other again.

I rise onto my toes, kissing him back. My hand fists his shirt as his mouth opens over mine, the kiss deepening. My back hits the counter. He lifts me easily, my legs wrapping around his waist. I gasp at the chill of the stone against my thighs, but the sound is swallowed by his mouth claiming mine again—hot and sure.

He unbuttons my pajama top with reverence, not haste. One button. Then another. His eyes flick up to mine with every inch of skin revealed. His lips follow his hands, grazing the swell of my breast, trailing heat down my ribs.

When his mouth closes over one nipple, I shiver and arch toward him, fingers tangled in his hair.

His other hand slides beneath the waistband of my pants, and I moan as he finds the place that's already aching for him. He moves slowly, intentionally, teasing me with every pass of his fingers. I clutch him tighter, already unraveling.

"God, I love how you fall apart for me," he murmurs against my skin, and I swear I see stars.

I grip his shoulders, breathless and trembling. "Then don't stop."

And he doesn't.

Not until I'm gasping, shaking, completely undone.

And even then—he stays.

Later, wrapped in his arms on the kitchen floor, I let myself believe it's safe to feel this much. To let love live here.

I want to belong to someone who never asked me to become anything but myself.

Because I'm not waiting for the other shoe to drop anymore.

I'm not falling.

I'm home.

# Chapter Twenty-Eight

Adam

The scent of cinnamon rolls and fresh coffee wraps around me like memory and hope all at once. I lean against the back counter of Christiane's diner—her dream made real—and try to process the fact that we made it. That *she* made it.

But it's not just hers anymore. It's ours. Every tile we scrubbed, every piece of reclaimed wood we sanded down and stained—every long night spent arguing about paint colors and pastry case placement—it's all *us*.

And still, she's fussing.

She's been up since before dawn, moving like a woman with purpose. But now, she stands still. Her hands flatten on the counter, and she scans the room with the same kind of stare I've seen her give wild hens or leaky faucets—like she's assessing the problem for a solution.

I move in behind her, sliding my arms around her waist and resting my chin on her shoulder. "You ready?" I murmur into her neck.

She doesn't answer immediately, just staring at the front door like it's the threshold between this dream and a disaster. "I hope so."

"You've already done the hard part, Chris. Now let them see it."

I press a kiss to her cheek and give her a soft nudge forward. She hesitates just long enough for me to feel the tremble in her breath, then reaches for the lock and flips the sign.

Open.

The bell above the door jingles. And just like that, they start pouring in.

Neighbors. Friends. A few skeptics whose names I know mostly from town meetings and grumbled warnings about how "some things just don't last." They enter slowly, cautiously. But one by one, their eyes soften. I watch how they take in the hand-painted menu, the copper light fixtures Christiane insisted we polish, the old black-and-white photo of her family framed by the pastry case.

It *feels* like home.

Christiane greets each guest like they're the only person in the room, and I can see her trying to hide the nerves behind that smile. Her hands fidget when she thinks no one's watching, but I'm always watching. I know how hard she worked for this. How terrified she was, it might all fall apart. Eli's the first to sit at the counter.

"Three cinnamon rolls and a plate of bacon, please," he says. "It's opening day, and I'm celebrating big."

Christiane laughs, shoulders loosening. "Don't choke on the icing."

By midmorning, the place is humming. Dishes clink, kids laugh, coffee brews steadily behind me, and Emmanuel is at the back door trying to break in because this is our life now.

"The goat's trying to unionize again," she calls out.

I smirk and head for the door. "He heard there were biscuits."

I drag him away before he headbutts through the glass. Someone snaps a photo. Laughter breaks out. Even Mr. Connors—who once told me over beers that she'd never last—grunts his approval over a plate of French toast and mutters, "Damn good eggs."

Just before lunch, the mayor shows up with a handshake and a proclamation that he'll be back "every Friday until I die." Then comes Mrs. Halverson, with a giant hug and tears in her eyes, insisting Christiane's lemon tarts taste just like the ones her mother used to make.

I hover behind the espresso machine, my heart swelling as I watch it unfold. This town wasn't built for outsiders, but somehow, she's carved out space for herself. She's not just surviving here—she's *belonging.* It rattles something deep in me. Something I didn't even know I was still guarding. The lunch rush finally slows enough for me to slip into the back. I find her leaning over the prep table, a little pale, breathing like she just ran a mile. There's no flour on her cheek—just exhaustion.

"You okay?" I ask, handing her a bottle of cold water.

She nods, but her eyes shimmer a little too brightly. "Just... a lot. I didn't think so many people would come."

I step closer, brushing my fingers down the side of her face. "They didn't just come for the food."

She gives me a wobbly smile. "I think I love it. All of it."

And I believe her. I believe her in a way that roots deep and true.

The rest of the day blurs—coffee refills, small talk, a tray dropped and quickly cleaned. Christiane floats through the room, her accent deepening when she gets excited, her laugh getting louder with each compliment. Every time our eyes meet, she grins like she's still not sure this is real. But it is. And it's *hers.*

When the bell over the door jingles one final time and the last guest leaves, the following silence is almost sacred. We clean side by side, her hair coming loose, her limp more pronounced, her apron dotted with chocolate and grease. She's exhausted. Glowing.

I slide a to-go box onto the counter and nudge it toward her.

"What's this?" she asks, lifting the lid.

Inside is a single croissant, carefully glazed with a tiny heart piped in raspberry. "You didn't think I was going to let the day end without one last bite of France, did you?"

She laughs, quiet and choked with something she doesn't say. Her eyes meet mine, and neither of us needs words for a second.

"You're good at this," she whispers.

"Only when it comes to you."

We settle into the window booth, legs stretched, shoes off, the sky outside melting into violet and rose. She leans her head on my shoulder, and I lace my fingers through hers. And as we sit in this little diner with the smell of butter and hope still hanging in the air, I realize something. The land mattered. The farm mattered. But this?

This is *home.*

Chapter Twenty-Nine
Christiane

When I drag myself out of bed the next morning, my legs ache like I ran a marathon, and my feet feel like they've been beaten with rolling pins. Every muscle is stiff, but I don't care.

Because yesterday the diner opened—and it was perfect.

Sunlight streams through the bedroom window, warming the patch of sheets where Adam was curled only an hour ago. I can hear him outside already—probably feeding the cattle or fixing the gate Emmanuel snapped again in his latest attempt to escape farm duty. I smile as I pad barefoot into the kitchen. The house is still and soft, humming with the afterglow of a dream realized.

I pull out a notepad and start scribbling ideas. Rotating seasonal specials. A honey-lavender tart for spring. A lemon crème brulé. Maybe a savory galette with local butternut squash. Dishes that whisper of France but speak in the voice of Willow Glen. The two no longer feel like separate parts of me. They've found a way to blend.

The screen door creaks open, and Adam steps inside, dusty and damp with early morning sweat. His hair is a tousled mess, his shirt half untucked. He looks like everything I never dared hope for.

"Morning, boss," he says, grinning.

I roll my eyes. "You're not on the payroll."

"Good," he replies, kissing my cheek on his way to the sink. "Because I hear your employees are underpaid and overworked."

I swat at him with the notepad, but warmth blooms in my chest. It's easy, this rhythm we've found—him teasing, me pretending not to smile. This little dance of ours.

Later that afternoon, the diner bell jingles—not with customers, but with a delivery. A massive bouquet of fall flowers wrapped in kraft paper, colors bursting in deep orange and golden yellow.

A simple card is tucked into the stems. *Congratulations on day one. We always knew you'd do it. Love, Margot.*

Tears sting my eyes. I blink them away and place the bouquet into a vintage milk jug, setting it front and center by the register. I run my fingers across the petals and silently thank her for still knowing exactly when I need reminding that I'm not alone.

By evening, the buzz around the opening hasn't faded. Mrs. Halverson returns with her grandkids and insists on trying everything from the breakfast menu—even though it's dinnertime. Eli practically claims the corner booth as his new second home. Everyone's already asking when we'll host a community dinner.

Just as I'm setting a slice of apple pie in front of Mr. Avery—one of the older farmers who still pays in exact change—he leans back and pats his belly.

"You know," Mr. Avery says, eyes twinkling as he sets down his fork, "we used to have a harvest supper right here in the square. Bonfires, cider, live music—the whole town came out."

I pause pie server in hand. "Really?"

He nods with a fond smile. "Yeah. Maggie's husband, Earl, used to organize the whole thing. She kept the diner running, but after he passed... well, the spark sort of went out. Nobody really picked it back up."

A few nearby customers chime in, their voices overlapping with sudden energy. Brandon suggests a hayride. Someone else mentions a pumpkin carving contest. Mrs. Halverson swears she still has the recipe for her famous spiced cider.

The momentum builds faster than I can keep up with, buzzing through the diner like a match to dry leaves.

The excitement builds faster than I can process it.

Adam slides in behind me, resting his hand lightly on the small of my back. "Sounds like you started something."

And just like that, the idea takes off.

Within days, we're planning an outdoor celebration. A potluck-meets-farmers'-market-meets-block-party. I agree to bake pies and supply cider from the diner. Local artisans volunteer to set up booths. Adam swears he can organize a hayride; someone even volunteers an old flatbed truck for it. There's talk of apple bobbing, pie-eating contests, and a pumpkin decorating table for kids.

Flyers go up. Volunteers sign up. The energy is contagious.

One afternoon, a little girl named Josie runs up to the counter and hands me a crayon drawing. In bold colors, she's scribbled a lopsided version of the diner, and a stick figure with wild brown hair stands smiling in the doorway.

"That's you," she says shyly, pointing to the drawing. "You make the best cookies."

I crouch down and thank her with a hug. I need it more than she does.

That night, I tape her drawing near the register beside Margot's flowers. I stare at the two together, this strange and beautiful mix of past and present, Paris and Willow Glen. And I don't feel like I'm balancing two halves. I feel whole.

A few days before the event, I'm outside stringing up lights across the front awning when I catch Adam watching me. He's leaning against the truck, arms crossed, his expression unreadable.

"What?" I ask, squinting at him through the glow of the lights.

He walks over and gently takes the spool from my hands. "Just thinking."

"About?"

"You. This place. All of it." He shrugs, eyes locked on mine. "It's hard to explain."

My heart stutters. I nod, letting him be quiet. I've learned not to push when he gets like this.

Because when Adam Williams looks at me that way—like I'm the only thing in the world that makes sense—it means something's coming.

I just don't know what yet.

Chapter Thirty

Adam

The town showed up.

I don't mean a few neighbors or the usual crowd who pop into the diner for coffee and gossip. I mean all of Willow Glen. Every street around the square is lined with cars, the sidewalks are packed, and the smells of cinnamon, woodsmoke, and roasted peanuts drift through the air like it's always belonged here.

And maybe it has. Maybe this festival didn't start with Christiane and me—but it's come back to life because of her.

I stand near the cider stand with Brandon, who's manning the tap and giving unsolicited dating advice to some poor teenager in a letterman jacket.

"This?" Brandon says, waving a plastic cup. "This is how you win hearts. You hand her a hot drink, smile just a little, and shut your damn mouth. Works every time."

The kid nods like he's been handed the secret to the universe.

"You're going to get someone arrested," I mutter.

Brandon shrugs. "Worked for me."

Patrick joins us, holding a half-eaten caramel apple. "You guys see Emmanuel? Someone said he's in the pumpkin patch."

I sigh. "Great."

"Relax," Patrick says. "He's a local celebrity now. Pretty sure Josie's been feeding him bites of funnel cake."

I glance around. There's live music coming from the gazebo. Kids painting gourds at the craft table. Mason jars glowing with floating candles line every walkway. And right in the center of it all is the diner—my girl's diner—lit up and warm, like a heartbeat in the middle of everything.

And I'm trying not to sweat through my flannel.

There's a box in my pocket. A question in my chest. And the kind of nerves I haven't felt since I stepped into my first county fair ring with a steer twice my size and nothing but pride to carry me through.

I make my way across the square, shaking hands and nodding to familiar faces.

"Williams," Mr. Avery calls from his folding chair, a wool blanket over his lap. "Tell your girl that pie she brought me was the best damn thing I've tasted since 1983."

"I'll let her know," I say, grinning.

"Don't wait too long to lock that one down," he adds, pointing his cane at me. "Women like her don't come around twice."

I nod, my throat suddenly too tight to answer.

I catch Josie near the pumpkin painting table, clutching a crooked gourd painted pink with sparkles. "I made this one for Miss Christiane," she announces proudly. "Because she's magic."

I ruffle her curls, my voice thick. "Yeah, she is."

Inside the diner, Christiane talks to the mayor and Mrs. Halverson, her hands flying as she tells a story. I linger near the door, just watching. There's flour on her cheek, and her braid's coming loose, but she's shining. She's absolutely shining.

There was a time I looked at Willow Glen like it owed me something. Tonight, I'm just grateful it gave me her.

When she catches me watching, her smile softens. She excuses herself and walks over.

"Hey," she says, brushing flour off her hands.

"Hey yourself. You've got a fan club outside."

She laughs. "I think Mr. Avery tried to proposition me with a sweet potato."

"I'm not surprised."

We stand together for a beat, breathing it in—the lights, the music, the community.

I tip my head toward the hayride wagon. "Want to sneak away?"

She eyes me. "That depends. Is there cider involved?"

"There's always cider."

She laughs again, and I tuck her hand into mine.

The night is only beginning. But I know where it ends.

And I know exactly what I will ask her when it does.

🐾🐾🐾

The back of the square is quieter. I lead her past the booths and lanterns to where we set up a bench near the tree line.

It's away from the glow and the bustle—just far enough to hear the music as a soft hum instead of a roar.

She exhales when we sit. "I didn't realize how loud it was until we stepped away."

I nod. My hands are in my jacket pockets, brushing against the small velvet box.

I've rebuilt barns and fenced fifty acres. But this—this tiny velvet box in my pocket—feels heavier than all of it combined.

"Remember when you first got here?" I say.

She smiles slowly. "Hard to forget. You were grumpy and impossible."

"I was," I agree, chuckling. "And you were a storm. Blew into my life and made a mess of everything I thought I had figured out."

She nudges my leg with hers. "You're lucky I like chaos."

I turn toward her, suddenly serious. "I was scared."

She stills. "Of me?"

"Of what you meant. Of what I could lose." I reach into my pocket and pull out the box. "But I don't want to be afraid anymore."

Her hand covers her mouth as I kneel, the box open between us.

"I love you. More than I ever thought I could love some-one. You made this place home. You made me better. And if you let me, I'll spend the rest of my life making sure you know just how much you mean to me."

Her eyes are wet. Her voice barely works. "Adam—"

"Marry me, Christiane."

She drops to her knees, laughing through her tears as she hugs me. "Yes. Of course, yes."

The ring is forgotten between us for a moment, caught between kisses and soft laughter and the way she says my name like it's her favorite word.

When I finally slip it onto her finger, it catches the glow of the lights from the square.

But she's the one who shines.

And for once, I don't feel like I'm chasing something I can't have.

I feel like I've finally come home.

Chapter Thirty-One
Christiane

The ring is heavier than I expected, not in weight but in meaning. It glints on my finger, catching the glow of the string lights as if it's tethered to the stars—as if it belongs there.

I haven't stopped staring at it since he slipped it on. We're still sitting in the grass, my knees damp and probably grass-stained, but I don't care. I don't think I could stand it if I tried. My whole body feels like it's vibrating with everything I can't quite say.

Adam watches me with that look of his; the one that sees through everything. And he still stays.

"I think my heart's going to fall out of my chest," I whisper.

He huffs a quiet laugh. "You didn't say anything when I gave it to you. I thought maybe I broke you."

I shake my head slowly, blinking hard. "I didn't say anything because I was trying not to sob."

And now that I've started talking about it, I can't stop.

"My mom's gone," I say, voice cracking. "Papa Mark's gone. And for so long, I thought I'd never have anyone again. I thought love was something I'd already used up."

Adam shifts closer, his hand finding mine, grounding me.

"But then you..." I laugh softly, brokenly. "You stomped into my life with your impossible attitude and your adorable dog and your damn flannel, and somewhere in the middle of all the fighting and baking and rebuilding barns, I started to believe again."

A tear slips down my cheek.

"I don't have a mother to cry with me over this ring. I don't have a father to walk me down the aisle. But I have you. And I have Margot. And I have this town that somehow let me belong again. And that's more than I ever dreamed I'd get back."

He cups my cheek with his rough hand, brushing away the tear with his thumb. "You don't have to carry any of it alone anymore."

I lean into his palm, eyes closing for just a second. Then I open them and look down at the ring again.

"It's beautiful," I whisper. "Simple. Real. Just like you."

He goes quiet. Then, softer, "It was my mom's."

I freeze, my heart thudding in my chest. "What?"

"She wore it for thirty-two years," he says, voice rougher now. "Said it wasn't about the size or the sparkle—it was about the weight of the promise behind it. She... she gave it to me before she passed. Told me I'd know when it was right."

I lift my hand again, staring at the ring as my eyes blur. "You're giving me her ring?"

He nods, "She would've liked you." Then, quieter, with a reverence that floors me, he says, "She would've loved you."

I'm crying before I realize it. I press my forehead to his, hands shaking. "Then I'll wear it like she's still with us."

And for a moment, I feel them—her, my *maman*, Papa Mark—all woven into this perfect night. Into this promise. Into us.

We stay there, quiet, until the music from the square shifts into something slow and familiar.

"Dance with me," I murmur.

"Here?"

"Here."

He stands first, offering his hand, and I take it. He pulls me into him, strong and steady, and we sway under the stars and the soft light spilling from the festival.

I rest my head against his chest. His heartbeat is steady, sure. And for the first time, I know I won't have to do this alone.

"I used to watch weddings," I whisper, "and tell myself I didn't need one. That I'd be fine on my own. Practical. Unattached. Safe."

Adam's arms tighten around me.

"But then you happened. And now I don't want safe. I want this."

When the music fades and the night grows cooler, we walk back hand-in-hand. My heart is light. Heavy too—but not with grief this time.

With hope.

Later, in the back office of the diner, I sit with the phone in my lap for five whole minutes before I call Margot. My hands still tremble. I almost don't do it. Saying it out loud makes it more real, and for a heartbeat, I'm afraid.

She answers on the second ring.

"You did it, didn't you?" she says.

I swallow. "He asked me."

"And you said yes."

"I did."

There's a pause. Then, gently, "*Maman* would be so proud of you."

That's when the dam breaks.

I cry. Ugly, hiccupping sobs that pull from a place I thought had gone quiet. Margot doesn't rush me. She just waits. Holds the space.

"She always said you'd be the strong one," Margot murmurs when I finally breathe again. "She said love would find you when you stopped chasing survival."

We talk for twenty minutes—about the proposal, town, and wedding. She offers to fly in, to help, to stand beside me. And when I hang up, I feel steadier.

Not patched. Not perfect.

But whole.

Back outside, Adam is leaning against his truck's hood, two cider mugs in hand. He passes one to me and kisses the top of my head.

"I want to marry you right here," I say quietly. "In the square. With string lights and pie and too much laughter."

He smiles, slow and sure. "Then that's what we'll do."

And just like that, our future starts to form—not from grand plans or perfect moments, but from this: the softness of cider steam, the warmth of a hand held, the promise of home.

One breath at a time.

Chapter Thirty-Two

Adam

I wake before the sun. The house is quiet, and the field is quieter still. Shadows stretch long across the grass, where the early morning dew clings like a blessing.

Today, I marry her.

The thought lands quiet and heavy like a stone dropped in deep water.

I sit on the edge of the bed and watch her sleep for a moment—soft, peaceful, curled on her side with the morning light just starting to touch her face. I think about all the mornings we'll have after this one. The routines. The slow coffees. The chaos. The quiet. I want it all.

My chest feels too tight. Not from dread, just the enormity of it all. For the first time, I'm not just holding something together. I'm building something new. And it scares the hell out of me in the best possible way. The clock ticks down. I shower. Shave. Put on the boots she says make me look like I own half the town—and maybe, after today, I will. Not by deed, but by heart. When Margot comes in to pin my boutonniere, she kisses my cheek and says something I don't understand in French, but I know it means I'm enough. And that's all I need.

I look down at the shirt and think about my Mom. She would've loved Christiane. She would've handed her a whisk and a photo album and called us family. Inside the house, Brandon shaves in the kitchen mirror and yells at Patrick for stealing his belt. They're loud. I wouldn't trade it for anything.

Patrick tosses me a box. "Vows?"

"Yeah," I mutter, opening the box and pulling out the folded sheet I wrote at two in the morning last night.

It took me hours. Not because I didn't know what to say. Because I wanted every word to carry the weight she deserves. She makes things feel possible, like forgiveness, starting over, planting something in the soil, and trusting it to grow.

I glance down at my hands. Still shaking slightly. But steady enough to hold hers when the time comes. Forty-five minutes later the square fills. I take the long way around the diner, checking the stage where we'll say our vows. It's simple—wooden beams wrapped with greenery and wildflowers. Nothing fancy. Just enough to frame the moment. For a second, I run my hand along the wood. I remember helping my dad set fence posts near the pasture—long before we knew we'd lose the land. I think about my mom and how she used to hum in the kitchen when she thought no one could hear. I wish they were here. I hope they'd be proud of the man standing here today.

People take their seats on bales of hay and mismatched chairs. It won't look like a magazine spread. It will look like us. Honest. Scrappy. Home.

The band tunes up. Emmanuel—God help us—is wearing a bow tie and trying to chew the corner of the guest book. Then the music shifts.

Everyone rises.

And there she is.

Walking down the aisle, bouquet in hand, sunlight in her hair. Her dress isn't huge or sparkly—it's simple. Elegant. Timeless. Like her. But it's the way she looks at me that nearly undoes me. Everything stills. Even the birds. Even me. She doesn't just walk toward me—she claims the space like it's always been hers. Like I have.

She reaches me and slides her hand into mine, steady as ever. And when I whisper, "You're the most beautiful thing I've ever seen," she leans in and says, "You're not so bad yourself, Williams."

We laugh. Then the officiant starts. The wind picks up slightly, enough to rustle the ribbon on her bouquet and the corner of my vow page. And then I speak.

"I used to think this town owed me something. I could fix the past by owning it—buy back the land, rebuild the barns, and bury the bitterness. But I didn't understand then that the only thing I ever needed... was someone to share it with. Someone who sees me. Who pushes back when I'm stubborn. Who bakes like a storm and kisses like peace."

Christiane's eyes shine.

"I promise to build with you. To rest with you. To weather every damn storm that comes for us. You made me believe in more, and I'll spend the rest of my life giving you everything I am."

She's crying. I'm close to crying. The whole town holds its breath.

The officiant gives us a pause, a quiet moment to breathe. She squeezes my hand, her thumb brushing the inside of my wrist. Like a promise already kept.

She opens her mouth and I realize—

She said yes weeks ago, but under these circumstances, with her last name about to be mine, I finally believe it. This isn't just a promise. It's proof. And then it's her turn.

Chapter Thirty-Three
Christiane

The breeze tugs at the ribbon on my bouquet, soft and insistent like it's urging me forward. My fingers tighten around Adam's. He's steady. Warm. Mine.

I look at him, and for a moment, I can't breathe. His dark hair is still damp at the temples. His jaw's freshly shaved, a nick just below his chin that wasn't there this morning. His eyes are locked on mine like there's nothing else he'd rather see in the world. The crowd disappears. The birds hush. Even the wind holds its breath.

He sees me. Not just the woman I am today, but all the pieces I used to be—the lost girl who buried three parents, the woman who ran, the woman who stayed. The one who chose him.

I didn't think I'd cry.

I was wrong.

My heart pounds beneath the lace bodice of my dress—so hard it feels like a second heartbeat, something wild and alive. I draw in a breath and start, my voice trembling but certain.

"When I came here, I was running from something," I say. "From grief. From failure. From the ache of wanting to belong somewhere and never quite fitting."

My eyes sweep over the crowd. I see Margot—tears tracking down her perfectly made-up face, her hands clasped tight in her lap. Patrick's boutonniere is crooked, no surprise there. Eli is pretending not to cry, failing miserably. Emmanuel is chewing on a bouquet ribbon in the back, looking too smug.

I smile through the tears.

"But this town didn't just give me a place to stay. It gave me you. A man who fought me from the start and still chose me anyway. A man who sees me—not the polished version I try to be—but the real me. Flaws, fears, fire, and all."

Adam's eyes shine. I feel his thumb brush the inside of my wrist—grounding me, anchoring me to this moment.

"You once told me you didn't know how to keep me," I whisper. "But the truth is... you never had to. I was already yours."

The wind picks up, tugging at my veil. It flutters behind me like wings.

"I vow to challenge you, to bake when words fail, and to meet you in every sunrise with gratitude. I vow to build with you a life and a home. One full of music, messes, morning coffees, and too many goats."

Laughter ripples through the crowd. Adam's shoulders shake with it, and I see how he looks at me like I just handed him forever.

"I vow to love you on the days it's easy and especially on the days it's not. Because real love isn't about perfection. It's about showing up. Again and again. It's about choosing each other every single day."

My voice cracks. I step forward and rest my forehead against his, eyes closed.

"You are the home I didn't know I was looking for. And I am so, so glad I found you."

The officiant clears their throat gently. "By the power vested in me by the great state of New York, and unofficially by the full approval of this town and its most mischievous goat... I now pronounce you husband and wife."

Adam doesn't wait. He kisses me like he's been holding his breath for years. The crowd erupts. Someone whoops. Eli whistles. Emmanuel bleats, likely in protest. But all I can hear is the catch in Adam's breath, the way his hand tightens at my waist like he means to never let go.

And just like that, we are married.

The reception is a blur of light and laughter. String lights flicker like fireflies. Mason jars clink with cider. Someone spills whipped cream down their shirt and still keeps dancing.

Margot tells a wildly exaggerated version of her first meeting with Adam during toasts, where I supposedly threw a croissant at Adam's head. I let her. I laugh until my ribs ache.

At one point, I catch a quiet moment, just the square and me. The grass is trampled. The tables are crooked. One of the dessert platters is empty, and Emmanuel is asleep under it like he earned a piece.

And it's perfect.

Later, Adam finds me by the cider table. His tie's half undone, his hair wind-tossed, and he's never looked more like mine.

He slides an arm around my waist. "You okay?"

I nod. "Just... memorizing."

He tugs me closer. "One more dance?"

I take off my shoes and nod. "Always."

We sway beneath the stars to a song I don't even remember hearing start. I press my face to his chest and listen to his heartbeat.

"You did it," he murmurs.

"We did it," I say. "Mr. Williams."

He grins. "Mrs. Williams."

I tilt my head back. "Still getting used to that."

"It looks good on you."

I kiss him again, slow and sure.

And for the first time, the word forever doesn't scare me.

It sounds perfect.

The dancing slows. The laughter fades into the background as guests drift home one by one. The square softens into quiet.

Adam's fingers stay laced with mine as we slip away from the glow of the string lights, just the two of us now. We end up behind the diner, where the sky stretches wide and dusted with stars.

He pulls me close, both of us swaying even though the music is long gone. My head rests against his chest, and the steady beat of his heart is a balm I didn't know I needed.

"You really okay?" he asks again, quieter this time.

I nod, then pause. "It feels like a dream. Like I'll wake up in that hotel room with nothing but flour under my nails and a passport I didn't know what to do with."

He tilts my chin up, eyes soft and serious. "You're not dreaming, Chris. You're home."

"I never thought I'd have this," I whisper. "Not really."

His thumb brushes the corner of my mouth. "Then we'll keep building it—brick by brick, croissant by croissant."

I laugh, and the tears come again, uninvited but welcome.

He leans in, forehead to mine. "You once said you were already mine," he murmurs. "But I want you to hear it from me now. I've been yours since you walked onto that porch and cursed me out in French."

My chest aches in the best way.

"I guess we were always heading here," I breathe.

"Yeah," he says. "But from now on—we walk it together."

And beneath the stars, with the scent of cinnamon still clinging to our skin and Emmanuel snoring somewhere under the cider table, I believe him.

We're not just starting something.

We've finally come home.

Chapter Thirty-Four
Adam

The cottage is quiet—the kind of quiet that seeps into your bones. Just the wind through the trees and the rhythmic crash of waves beyond the dunes. The ocean is right outside, but I haven't looked at it once.

Not when she's standing there, barefoot and beautiful, silhouetted in the golden spill of light from the window. Her dress is rumpled from the drive, and her hair falls in soft brown waves like it was made to be touched. She doesn't turn. She just stands there, letting me look.

"You keep staring," she says.

I set the suitcase down and cross the room, wrapping my arms around her from behind. "Can you blame me?"

She leans into me, warm and soft, and I swear I have never been so content.

"We're really married," she murmurs.

"We are."

She turns to face me, and everything slows. Her eyes, bright and shining, hold something I've never had from her before—unfiltered trust. I cup her cheek, brushing my thumb over her bottom lip.

"I brought lingerie," she says, half smiling like it's a confession.

I groan low in my throat. "You could wear a flannel sack, and I'd still be on my knees."

She rolls her eyes, but the curve of her mouth deepens. "You do have a thing for flannel."

"I have a thing for you."

She doesn't get a chance to reply before I lift her into my arms. She laughs, surprised, wrapping herself around me with an instinctual grace. I carry her to the bed slowly, carefully, reverently and set her down like she's something breakable. Because under all the strength, I know how tender she really is. And I'll spend my whole life protecting that softness.

Her dress slips off her shoulders easily. I watch it fall, pooling at her waist. She's sitting there in lace and nothing else, skin kissed with freckles and lit by sunset gold. My mouth goes dry.

"Say something," she whispers, suddenly shy.

I close the space between us. "I've never wanted anything more."

My mouth finds hers—hungry, claiming. She tastes like heat and cinnamon and forever. Her hands fumble with my shirt, buttons scattering, her touch bold but shaking.

"You're mine now," she says against my lips.

"I always was."

She shoves the fabric from my shoulders, her hands skimming down my chest like she's relearning me. I growl at her touch low, guttural. Her nails leave trails down my stomach, and I swear under my breath.

When I lift her, she gasps. When I lay her back, she moans.

"Take your time," she whispers.

So I do.

I kiss her like it's the first time. Like I've waited years. Like this is holy. And maybe it is.

I trace her collarbone with my lips. The swell of her breast. The dip of her stomach. When I finally settle between her thighs, she arches up, breath catching, a shiver rippling through her. I tease her with my tongue, reveling in her heat and wetness. Knowing it is all for me, because of me. Nipping her thighs with my teeth, I can't help but grin at her pleas for more.

She says my name like it's the only one she knows, and I plan to keep it that way for the rest of our lives. Sliding up her body, I snag her lips with mine, and she wraps her arms around my neck. I use two fingers to tease her entrance before sliding them deep, curving slightly to hit that one spot that drives her crazy. And when she comes apart, it's not quiet. It's a symphony. And it belongs to me.

When I move between her legs, she pulls me closer, her legs wrapping around me like she never wants to let go.

"I want all of you," she breathes.

"You have me," I promise. Lining the head of my cock with her entrance, I sink in one inch at a time, and the moan that escapes my chest is almost desperate. I move slowly at first, taking my time to savor this moment, the very first moment when we are joined together as man and wife. Christiane is gasping beneath me, her breath hot on my neck as she nips at my shoulder.

"Faster," Christiane pants beneath me, her pupils blown wide as she stares up at me.

"Faster?" I hitch her leg up to adjust my angle, and she moans in response to the change in angle.

"Faster." She sounds so sure. Who am I to deny my wife anything? Reaching up, I grab the headboard with one hand for leverage and start to thrust harder and faster. This time when she falls apart under me, I join her.

🐾

Staring out the open patio doors of the cottage with Chris curled up on my chest is my new version of heaven. I glide my fingers up and down her arms, and she chuckles. "When we first met nine months ago, did you think we would be here?"

I take a deep breath and hold it for a minute as I reflect on the last nine months and the days we first met. "Maybe not consciously, but I have loved you since I first met you. I was just so stubborn about getting out of my own way."

"Jeez, Williams, I already married you. Calm down." She's teasing me, and I kiss the top of her head, grinning like a lunatic.

"Yes. Yes, you did. No take-backs, returns, or exchanges."

"I wouldn't dream of it." She yawns before cuddling closer. I pull up the flannel blanket from the foot of the bed and just hold her as she naps nestled onto my chest.

🐾🐾🐾

I'm not sure what wakes me at first. The sun is setting over the waves, and for a moment, I forget where I am, but then I feel a warm mouth close around the head of my shaft, and I am fully awake. Chris's mouth is the best alarm clock on the planet. "Can I help you, wife?"

"I woke up feeling neglected, so I decided to have some fun." Her tongue swirling around me makes me think her definition of fun and mine might be something totally different.

"Seems to me you just want to play. If you wanted my attention, all you had to do was ask." When she takes me to the back of her throat in one stroke, I can't help but arch my back and moan. Her mouth feels like heaven, but fuck, it is pure sin.

"I tried to wake you, but you must've been having the dream of your life. He was already upright and begging for attention. How could I refuse?" Her tone is playful and sultry, and I get to hear her for the rest of my life.

Lucky me.

"Well, I am awake now, and if you're done teasing, I am more than happy to tell you exactly how much I loved my wake-up call."

Chris climbs up my body, her hand still firmly wrapped around my cock. "What did you have in mind exactly? Because I have to tell you, I'm having a pretty good time right now."

"Right now, all I want to do is flip you onto your back and—"

She arches a brow, teasing. "And?"

I grin, already easing her down beneath me.

"And make sure you remember this for the rest of your damn life."

And then I prove it. With every stroke, every kiss, every whispered vow carved into her skin.

We move together, slow and sure. This isn't the frantic kind of love. This is the kind that knows. That chooses. That keeps choosing.

Later, when we're tangled in sheets, breath, and laughter, she rests her head on my chest and traces lazy circles over my skin.

"This place is perfect," she says.

"You're perfect," I answer, kissing her temple.

She hums, content, eyes already drifting shut.

Outside, the ocean sings. Inside, I have everything I ever wanted.

And I'm never letting go.

Chapter Thirty-Five
Christiane

The sheets still smell like salt and skin.

Adam's breathing is deep and even beneath me, his fingers trailing idle patterns across my back. We haven't said much in the last few minutes but don't need to. There's a language between us now—quiet, sure, and deeply felt.

I shift slightly, just enough to press my ear over his heart. I can feel it, steady and strong. Mine. My husband.

We're married.

God, how is this real?

I never thought I'd have this. Not with someone like him. Not with someone who sees me, really sees me, even the parts I used to flinch away from in the mirror. And yet here

I am. A little sore. A lot in love. Wrapped up in a man who holds me like I'm his peace.

A soft breeze dances through the open window. The scent of the ocean carries with it the sound of distant waves and the faint cry of gulls. It's peaceful in a way I didn't know I needed until now.

Adam shifts under me, murmuring something low and half asleep. I smile against his skin.

This isn't the honeymoon I imagined—not that I ever imagined one. But it's exactly right. A warm, private world carved out just for us. No expectations. No obligations. Just the two of us, skin to skin, soul to soul.

Eventually I push myself up just enough to look at him. His eyes are closed, lashes dark against his cheek, jaw shadowed and kissed by the sun. He seems younger like this. Softer.

I kiss the corner of his mouth and slip out of bed. He doesn't stir. I don't mind. He carried us through most of today. I can let him rest.

As I pad through the little cottage, the wood floors are cool under my feet. Everything about this place feels like him. Warm. Sturdy. Safe.

I find a blanket, one of those chunky knit ones that smells faintly of lavender, and step out onto the deck. The ocean is painted in strokes of silver and indigo, the last bits of sunlight dancing across the water like fireflies. I curl up in one of the chairs and pull the blanket around me.

It's strange, this stillness. For months now, everything's been moving—so fast, so chaotic. But now? It's quiet. And it's not empty.

It's full.

Of love. Of him. Of the life we're building.

I run my fingers over the band on my left hand, the gold cool and solid against my skin. I still can't quite believe it's real.

But it is.

We are.

🐾🐾🐾

I wake to the smell of something... burning.

Smoke, not heavy—just enough to raise a brow. There's also the distinct sizzle of bacon and a string of creative cursing from the kitchen.

I roll over to find the bed empty, rumpled with the ghost of Adam's warmth. Pulling on one of his flannels, I pad down the hallway barefoot and peer into the kitchen.

He's standing over the stove shirtless, hair a mess, with a spatula in one hand and a smoking pan in the other. There's flour on his jaw and what looks suspiciously like pancake batter on his shoulder.

"Don't even think about it," he says without turning around. "I've got this."

"Clearly," I murmur, leaning against the doorframe with a smirk.

He finally looks over, and despite the chaos, he grins. "Sit. Drink your coffee. You're not lifting a finger. I'm making you breakfast."

Bless him, my mug is already on the counter, and I take a sip while watching him try to flip a pancake that has definitely fused with the pan.

"Was the spatula supposed to be part of the pancake?" I ask, sipping slowly.

"Absolutely," he says, deadpan. "Adds texture."

I giggle, warm and content. "You're determined."

"I'm your husband. It's literally in the vows—'love, honor, and at least try not to burn the bacon.'" He waves the spatula triumphantly. "Now sit and let me court disaster in peace."

I do, letting him clatter and sizzle his way through it. The pancakes are questionable. The bacon is crisp, maybe too crisp. But when he sets the plate in front of me with a proud look on his face, I beam.

"Perfect," I lie, taking a bite.

He watches me chew with suspicious intensity. "Is it... edible?"

"It's made with love," I say, chewing carefully. "And enough enthusiasm to mask any and all culinary crimes."

He laughs, sliding into the seat across from me. "Fair enough."

I set my fork down and smile. "What if we went into town? Got breakfast at that little diner you keep talking about. Did some shopping. Just... wandered."

He perks up instantly. "You mean get out of this perfect love nest and interact with actual humans?"

"Only a few. For a short while. Then we can come back and lock the door and resume honeymoon activities."

"Say no more. I'll get the keys."

Briar Sound is quiet on Sunday mornings. The shops open late, people stroll slowly, and everything smells like coffee and cinnamon rolls. We wander hand-in-hand past the bookstore, a little bakery, and a store with antique dishware I swear I *don't* need, but we still wander into it for fifteen minutes.

It's peaceful. Until it's not.

Because that's when the goat comes flying down Main Street. A little cream-colored blur barrels past the post office, pursued by a pack of giggling children. Her ears are flapping, hooves scrambling for traction, and her bleat sounds downright gleeful.

"What the—" Adam blinks as the goat rounds the corner and heads straight for us.

She doesn't slow down.

"Catch her!" one of the kids yells. "She stole Mrs. Lottie's muffin!"

"She what?"

But before we can process it, the goat skids to a stop and then launches herself directly at Adam. He catches her on instinct, stumbling a step back as she settles in his arms like she belongs there. She smells like frosting and mischief.

Christ.

"Is this normal?" I ask, reaching out to steady them both.

"No," a breathless little boy says, skidding to a stop in front of us. "But she does this a lot. The whole town's been trying to catch her for months. Nobody knows where she came from, but she keeps escaping pens and stealing baked goods. We call her Muffin."

"Muffin," I repeat, rubbing behind her ear. She leans into my hand like she approves. "That tracks, but she looks like an Emma to me."

Adam looks at me, then back at the goat. "You thinking what I'm thinking?"

"I'm thinking she's a menace."

"Exactly. She'll fit right in."

Emma is curled up in a blanket in the backseat like she owns the place. Adam keeps glancing in the rearview mirror and laughing to himself.

"We went out for shopping," he says. "Came home with a goat."

"Newlywed things," I say, smiling as I squeeze his hand.

Home is waiting. And now, apparently, so is a goat.

Chapter Thirty-Six

Adam

The second the truck's tires crunch over the gravel drive, tension I didn't know I was carrying slips loose. The farm's not flashy—hell, half the fence still leans like it's had too much whiskey—but it's ours. Every inch of it. After a week of ocean breeze and wild honeymoon mornings, I didn't think I'd be ready to come back.

Turns out, I was dead wrong.

Christiane yawns beside me, soft and sleepy, her fingers absently resting on the tiny cream menace curled up in the seat like she was born to ride shotgun.

Emma.

Yeah, the name changed between the shop and the local diner. Apparently, "Muffin" wasn't dignified enough for the tiny thief chewing absently on one of my flannel blankets. I glance down at her next to me. She blinks. I swear she smirks.

"We're home," I say.

Christiane stretches, then smiles that sleepy smile that always does me in. "Do you think Emmanuel will behave?"

"Absolutely not," I say. "But I've missed the little menace."

We park, and the front porch creaks before I can even open Christiane's door. Emmanuel materializes like a ghost with a vendetta, head high, tail twitching like he already knows he's been replaced. The moment he sees the goat in our backseat, he freezes.

Then snorts.

Then charges.

"Nonononono—" I sprint around the truck just as Emma bolts out behind Christiane's legs, bleats once, and launches herself onto the porch like she's been here her whole life. They collide—not hard, but loud enough to make me wince. Emmanuel reels like someone just insulted his lineage. Emma stares at him, cool as ice, her little cream tail flicking like a queen waving off her court.

Christiane doubles over, laughing, clinging to the truck door. "Oh my God. She just—did you see that? She checked him."

"I saw," I mutter, watching the standoff unfold. "She's got guts. He's not gonna know what hit him."

Emmanuel snorts again and trots off, chest puffed, pretending it didn't happen. Emma trots after him like she owns the place.

Knowing our track record with animals, she probably will by the end of the week. We've unpacked half our bags and already been headbutted twice. Emma has claimed the corner of the barn where the sun hits in the afternoon. Emmanuel's sulking under the old tractor and refusing to make eye contact.

"Should we be worried?" I ask, watching from the porch as Emma sniffs around the fence line.

Christiane leans into my side. "About the goat hierarchy?"

"About the fact that our animals are more dramatic than most people."

She snorts. "You love it."

I do. I really, really do. I pull her close, chin settling on the crown of her head like it's always belonged there. "It's good to be home."

"It is."

We stand there a long time. Watching the wind roll through the fields, feeling the kind of peace that only comes when you've earned it. Inside, the farmhouse is warm and lived-in. It smells like cinnamon, wood polish, and the last dregs of honeymoon candle wax.

Outside, Emma lets out a victorious bleat as she hops onto the porch swing.

"God help us," I mutter.

Christiane just laughs. "Welcome to married life, Williams. We've got goats and chaos and probably a thousand unfinished chores."

I grin, pressing a kiss to her temple. "And I wouldn't trade a damn thing."

🐾🐾🐾

The sun's starting to dip low, throwing long shadows across the pasture as I run my hand along the fence line. It's still a little crooked in places, but it holds. That's what matters. I shift a loose board back into place and grab a nail from the pouch on my hip. The hammer—passed down from my dad—is worn smooth from years of use, and it fits in my hand like it belongs there. A few quick swings and the board settles where it should.

It's nothing fancy. Just a fence. Just a barn. Just a hundred little pieces of a life I never thought I'd get to have. I lean back and let my eyes sweep over it—our land. Scraped together with stubborn hope and more than a bit of sweat. Every broken fencepost. Every patch of overgrown field. All of it *ours*.

Christiane's still inside, probably chasing Emma off the kitchen table. I'd offer to help, but honestly? This is the quiet I didn't realize I'd missed. The honeymoon was perfect—beaches and flannel blankets and morning sex that turned into afternoon sex and then late-night giggles under the covers—but this right here?

This is the good stuff.

Sweat down my back. Dust on my boots. The scent of hay and woodsmoke curling on the air. I can see Emmanuel sulking under a tree. Emma's not far off, chewing on what might have once been my hat.

God help us.

I wipe my hands on my jeans and rest my arms on the top rail. The breeze cuts gently across the field, the late-summer air that hints at fall. I think about Christiane—curled up in the truck, drowsy and content, her hand drifting to her stomach like she was guarding something sacred. She doesn't even realize she's doing it.

I shake my head. It's probably nothing. Still... something about how she's been lately—soft, thoughtful, almost glowing—makes me wonder. I glance back toward the farmhouse. The lights are on. The windows glow warm against the dusk. This place... it's more than a home. It's a beginning.

"Adam!" Her voice floats through the dusk, warm and easy—like home calling me in by name. "Dinner's ready!"

I turn, and there she is—framed by the doorway, apron on, hair up in a messy knot, and smiling like I'm the only thing she sees. "On my way," I call back, grabbing the hammer and slinging it over my shoulder. I head toward the porch, hammer over one shoulder, Emmanuel stalking at my heels like a grumpy chaperone. Emma bounces along behind him, all attitude and tiny hooves. The sky burns gold behind the barn, and for the first time in a long damn time, everything feels exactly right.

Her. This land. This messy, perfect life.

And deep down, something tells me—we're only at the beginning.

Chapter Thirty-Seven
Christiane

The diner smells like cinnamon rolls, bacon, and something I can't quite identify—and my stomach turns in protest. Not queasy. Not unsettled. *Revolted.* The kind of gut-deep no that makes my fingers curl around my water glass just to ground myself. Across from me, Adam is blissfully unaware, digging into a stack of waffles like they personally insulted his mother.

"You okay?" he asks between bites, syrup clinging to the corner of his mouth. "You've barely touched your toast."

I force a smile, trying to breathe through it. "Yeah. Just... not super hungry today."

His brow furrows. That soft, silent concern he does so well. He doesn't press, but he watches me closer now. I hate how well he knows me.

"That's the third time this week," he says, voice gentle but laced with curiosity.

"Maybe I'm getting a cold," I lie, pushing the plate away.

He nods, but I can feel him filing that response away. He's been doing that a lot lately—watching me from the corner of his eye when I sit too long with my hand on my belly. When I wince at smells I used to love. When I fall asleep before we've even turned the porch lights off. I glance toward the counter where Mrs. Dorsey is refilling coffee, then out the window toward the little pharmacy across the street. Something sharp coils low in my gut—tension, dread, hope.

Because deep down, I already know.

The missed period, the exhaustion that doesn't touch my bones, it *owns* them. The way my body feels like it's shifting around something invisible, something growing. I press my palm lightly to my stomach under the table. No curve. No sign. Just... a knowing.

"I think I need to stop by the pharmacy on the way home," I say suddenly, grabbing my purse like a lifeline. "Can we take our food to go?"

Adam blinks, surprised. "Uh, yeah. Sure. Everything okay?"

"Yeah," I say again, too fast. My voice doesn't match my hands—they're shaking as I brush a kiss against his cheek. "Just need to check on something."

🐾🐾🐾

The test sits on the counter like it *knows*. I pace the bathroom like that will make time move faster, like walking tiny laps over worn tile will keep me from unraveling. Outside the window, the wind rustles the trees and scatters leaves across the porch. I can hear Emma bleat from somewhere near the barn. Emmanuel answers with dramatic flair, like always.

Their world hasn't shifted. Mine just might.

The timer buzzes.

My hand hovers over the test. I don't breathe. I just... stare.

Please don't let me be wrong. I pick it up.

Two pink lines.

The world doesn't stop—but my heart does. For one beat. Two. Then it kicks back in all at once, crashing against my ribs like it's trying to escape. My knees give. I sit on the tub's edge and cover my mouth with one hand.

I'm pregnant.

The words land like a whisper inside me, slow and warm and terrifyingly beautiful. Tears well in my eyes. Slow at first, then faster, until they're dripping down my chin and I'm laughing through the blur.

"I'm pregnant," I say again, softly, into the room's quiet. My hand drifts to my belly, flat and still so *mine*—but no longer just mine. There's someone else in there now. Tiny. Forming. Real.

A part of Adam. A part of me.

Ours.

For a long moment, I let myself feel joy, fear, wonder, a wild flutter of love that feels too big for this tiny room. Then I wipe my face, clutch the test in one hand, and bolt for the door.

Ten minutes later I find Adam by the chicken coop, sleeves rolled up, coaxing one of the hens out of a bucket. There's dirt on his forearms, his hair a little too wild, and he's humming to himself like he hasn't just changed my entire life.

He turns when he sees me, his expression instantly alert. "Hey, are you okay? You've been gone a while."

I stop a few feet from him, breath catching.

There's no *perfect* way to say it. No script.

So I just say it.

"I took a test."

He goes still, one hand still buried in the feed bin. "Yeah?"

My voice shakes. "I'm pregnant."

Everything in him stills then comes alive all at once. He blinks. Breathes. And then crosses the space between us like the earth's spinning too fast without me in his arms.

He grabs me and wraps me in the safest, strongest hug I've ever felt.

"You're..." He leans back just far enough to see my face. "You're *sure*?"

I nod, tears slipping down my cheeks again. "Two pink lines."

He pulls me in tighter, his hand cradling the back of my head. His voice is hoarse, trembling. "We're having a baby?"

I nod again. "We are."

His shoulders shake. Not with laughter. Not quite with tears. Just... with everything.

He pulls back again, eyes red, smile wide. "Holy shit."

I laugh, breathless. "Right?"

"Are you okay? You're not too sick? Do you need—God, do we have crackers? I can get—"

"Adam."

He stops mid-ramble.

"I'm okay. And yes, I'll take some crackers later."

His hand comes to my stomach like a question. I take it, press it there. "There's a baby in there," he whispers, almost reverent.

"There is." A beat passes. Then another. I bite my lip, heart full to bursting. "If it's a girl... I want to name her Susanne. After my mom."

Adam's eyes shine. "I love that. She'd be proud."

"And if it's a boy..." My voice softens. "I'd like to name him after your grandfather."

He stills. A long breath escapes him. "Michael?"

I nod. "Michael."

He presses his lips to my forehead, my cheek, and finally to my mouth—slow and deep, full of every unsaid thing. When we pull apart, I'm smiling so hard my cheeks ache.

"We're really doing this," I whisper.

"We are," he says. "God help us."

Chapter Thirty-Eight

Adam

The farmhouse smells like cinnamon, woodsmoke, and something vaguely burned that I'm not asking questions about. Pregnancy's done a number on Christiane's sense of smell. Cloves make her gag. Garlic is a federal offense. Cinnamon? That one's unpredictable. She claims it's fine until it isn't, and suddenly, I'm the enemy for lighting a candle.

Last week, she tried baking muffins—*tried* being the key word. I walked into the kitchen to find blackened sugar crusted on the bottom of the oven, the fire alarm still swinging from where she'd swatted it with a broom and her crying into a mixing bowl like it had personally betrayed her. I stood there like an idiot, unsure if I should grab the broom or the baking tray or just quietly leave the room. I didn't even get a word out before she burst into fresh tears, sobbing that she'd "ruined breakfast and possibly Christmas." I had no idea what to do with that—except wrap my arms around her and hope it was enough.

I held her for twenty minutes, promised to buy store-bought muffins for the rest of our lives, and told her she was beautiful, emotional, and a little terrifying. She laughed through the tears. Then she made French toast instead. Burned that too. Now I don't ask. I keep a fire extinguisher in the pantry and pretend not to notice the scorch marks on the bottom of the cookie sheet.

There's a wreath on the door. Twinkle lights on the mantel. Emmanuel is wearing a red plaid bowtie, which he keeps trying to chew off. Emma—God help me—has antlers strapped to her head like she's auditioning for the world's most chaotic Christmas pageant. And somehow, in the middle of all this madness, I've never felt more at home. Christiane stands barefoot near the tree, stringing popcorn garland with her tongue sticking out slightly in concentration. Five months pregnant, glowing, and entirely fixated on making everything *just right*. She hums under her breath as she works; something slow and old, French maybe. Probably one of her mom's songs.

She pauses, one hand on her belly, the other reaching for an ornament shaped like a goat in a Santa hat.

"She's kicking," she says softly without looking up.

My feet move before I think. I kneel beside her and press my palm gently against the curve of her belly. I feel a soft flutter, like a knock from the inside.

"Hey, little one," I whisper. "Your mom wants to adopt a cow. Just wait until you meet the goats."

Christiane laughs, eyes shining. "You'll love her. She's perfect."

I look up at her, already knowing I've lost. "You're serious about this."

"She's perfect," she says again, grinning now as she walks over and grabs her laptop. She spins the screen around. "Her name's Nessa. Look at that face."

I squint. The cow is... fluffy. And tiny. And I'll admit—pretty damn cute.

"Christiane," I say carefully, stepping into the room. "You are five and a half months pregnant."

"Exactly," she says as if I just made her point. "And I want her here before the baby comes."

I sit down beside her and glance at the listing again. It's a small farm in Piper Falls, Texas. At least a twenty-five-hour drive, maybe more with snow. "You want me to drive halfway across the country. In December. While you're pregnant. To pick up a cow."

"A *mini* cow," she corrects. "And it's not like I'm asking to drive. I was hoping you would."

I raise an eyebrow. She gives me her best sweet-angel smile—the one that has historically made me forget how to say no. "It would mean a lot to me."

I let out a long breath and scrub a hand over my face. "You're lucky I love you."

"I know."

I close the laptop and pull her into my lap carefully. She curls against me, belly warm against my chest, and I press a kiss to her temple. "I don't want you on the road for days, especially not in winter. Too many things could go wrong."

"I'm fine," she murmurs into my neck. "The doctor said everything's going perfectly."

"I know." I rest my hand over her bump. "But I'm not taking any chances with you. Or with this little one."

She huffs, then chuckles. "So what—you're going to teleport her here?"

"Nope," I say, reaching for my phone. "I'm going to call Patrick."

Patrick is staring at me like I've grown antlers myself. "You want me to drive to *Texas* to pick up a cow?"

"A mini Highland cow," Christiane chirps helpfully from the other room.

He blinks. "Named Nessa?"

"She's got bangs," I offer. "Apparently, that's a selling point."

Patrick tilts his head. "Is this what happens when you get married? You start collecting goats and pocket-sized livestock like trading cards?"

"Pretty much."

He leans against the doorframe, one hand on his hip. "And this... assignment. Is this because I owe you for helping me move that busted canoe last spring?"

"Partially. Also, you're the only one I trust to handle the cow and the truck and not come home with a DUI or an alpaca instead."

He snorts. "Can't make promises. Might depend on how much moonshine they're offering in Texas."

I hand him a piece of paper with directions, a down payment receipt, and a detailed list of things Christiane insists the cow needs. He reads it, his eyebrows rising. "She has a *grooming brush preference?*"

"She's got standards."

Christiane peeks around the corner. "Don't let her get cold."

Patrick groans. "If I die on this trip, I hope you name the baby after me."

"Only if it's a girl," I call back.

He flips me off on his way out the door, muttering something about ridiculous farmers and high-maintenance cows. The door clicks shut, and Christiane stays wrapped around me for a while, her chin tucked against my shoulder. I hold her tighter—not because I have to, but because I want to. Because I still can't quite believe this is real.

A year ago, I didn't have any of this. No goats. No antler-wearing chaos. No woman humming French lullabies while stringing popcorn garland. No baby kicking under my palm.

Now? It's everything.

She exhales against me, warm and content. "You didn't have to do that."

"I kind of did," I murmur, turning to kiss the edge of her jaw. "Because if you wanted a damn dragon, I'd find a way to bring one home."

Chapter Thirty-Nine

Patrick

By the time I hit the edge of Piper Falls, Texas, I've survived six states, four gas station coffees, two dodgy burritos, and precisely one existential crisis in a Dairy Queen parking lot. The GPS cheerfully tells me I'm ten minutes out. My back tells me I'm seventy years old.

Somewhere in Arkansas, I lost faith in humanity. Somewhere in Tennessee, I remembered I don't even like cows. And yet here I am, fifty hours in, driving a borrowed truck with hay scattered across the back seat and a playlist full of murder podcasts because silence made the "why am I doing this" question too loud.

All this... for a cow.

If she doesn't greet me with a thank-you card and a warm nuzzle, I swear I'll leave her at the first rest stop with a note.

The gravel drive winds past a pasture full of shaggy Highland cattle. One of them—Nessa, I assume—is sprawled under a tree like a spoiled heiress in a fur coat. Nearby, a much larger one with crooked horns and serial-killer eyes is attempting to headbutt a gate latch open.

Fantastic. There's always one.

I park beside a red barn and kill the engine. No one comes out.

"Cool," I mutter. "Kidnap a cow, fall off the grid. Classic."

I'm halfway through the barn door when a voice cuts through the shadows—low, sharp, and unmistakably Scottish.

"If ye drag any more mud into this barn, I'll pelt ye square in the face wi' a bucket."

I freeze.

At the far end of the aisle stands a woman in boots, a worn shirt tied over a white tank, and jeans dusted with hay. She's small but fierce, with red hair braided over one shoulder and hands on her hips like she owns the place—or would die defending it.

"I'm Patrick," I say, lifting my hands. "I'm here for Nessa?"

She eyes me like I might be contagious. "You're early."

"You're Scottish."

"Aye, and you've got ears. We're off tae a crackin' start."

I blink. "You're the... owner?"

She snorts. "Hardly. Place belonged tae my stepdad. I'm just the unlucky sod left tae sort the whole bloody mess."

She crosses the barn, grabs a clipboard, and gives me a once-over like she's still deciding whether I'm worth the effort. "The coo's no' ready."

"She's not ready?"

"She's moody," she says, as if that clears everything up. "And if I push her, she'll bolt like Dougal did last week, and you'll be chasing her through the fields in boots that scream bad decisions."

"Dougal?"

She nods toward the pen behind her. "That big numpty in the corner. Thinks he's clever. He's no'. Just misunderstood wi' a talent for poor life choices and an arse like a batterin' ram."

I peer inside. The massive Highland cow is chewing on a feed bucket, unbothered, while slowly inching his backside toward the stall gate like he's plotting an escape.

"Jesus."

"Aye," she says with a sigh. "He means well. He just doesnae think things through."

I glance toward the pasture and notice a section of fence
sagging like it gave up halfway through the workday.

"You know your fence is falling down?"

"Aye. Things keep breakin' lately," she mutters. "The tractor, the boiler, gate hinges, that corner post. Dougal tried
tae sit on it like a stool."

"Tough time to be managing a farm alone."

Her mouth twitches—just a flicker of something tired
beneath the steel. "Tell me about it."

But she shrugs it off like she's used to carrying more than
her share. "You'll stay the night. Nessa's no' leavin' till she's
good and ready."

"Do I at least get a bed?"

"There's a guest cabin. No telly. No Wi-Fi. No whinin'."

"This is starting to sound less like a pickup and more like
a hostage situation."

"Only if you scream," she says sweetly, already striding
away.

I follow her because what else do you do when the woman
in charge of your cow looks like she'd bite if cornered—and
somehow still smells like hay and something floral?

"This how you treat all your visitors?"

She glances back. "Only the ones who show up early and act like they've never seen a coo wi' opinions."

"What exactly do cows with opinions need before a long drive?"

She stops. "Space. Patience. A handler who doesnae act like a tourist."

I cross my arms. "I grew up on a farm."

"With cattle, aye? Angus or somethin' like that. Explains the dead eyes and the misplaced confidence."

"I didn't realize you'd done a full background check."

"Didn't have tae. One look at ye, and I knew. You're the helper friend."

That catches me off guard. "The what?"

"The kind that always gets roped in tae help clean up someone else's disaster. Fetch the supplies. Move the furniture. Drive across the country for a coo that looks better in a tuxedo than you do."

My mouth opens. Closes. "Okay. That's... weirdly accurate."

She shrugs. "Lucky guess."

Her smirk is trouble. So is the gleam in her eye. And for a moment, I forget why I'm here.

"I'm Patrick," I repeat because it's the only thing I can think to say.

She sighs, but it's not unfriendly. "Mharie. Welcome tae Highland Homestead."

I glance around—the sagging fence, the cow-proof trailer I should've insisted on, and the oversized ginger cow currently trying to sneak out of his stall backward.

"You sure it's not the other way around?"

She shrugs. "Could be."

On the walk back toward the yard, I steal another glance at her. Fierce posture, sharp tongue, that fire in her eyes. Not so different from the way Christiane looked when she first landed in Willow Glen—feisty, yes, but sad too. Adam had been an ass about it, and I was caught between them, trying to keep the peace while wondering if Christiane might break under the weight of it all.

And maybe that's why I can't shake the feeling here. Mharie's grieving, angry at the world, and left holding the bag on a place that means everything to her but isn't hers yet. I don't know her from anyone, but she's got that same raw edge of someone who's been handed too much.

Not that I came here by choice. Adam guilted me into it—reminded me how much it'd mean to Christiane to have

Nessa at Willow Glen by Christmas. So I packed up, hit the road, and told myself it was just a favor. A quick pickup. A handoff. Done.

But standing here, watching Mharie mutter what I assume are Scottish curses while Dougal rams the fence again, I'm starting to wonder if maybe fate had other ideas.

I clear my throat. "So, this guest cabin... does it come with sheets or am I about to learn how authentic Texas camping feels?"

She shoots me a sidelong glance, lips twitching. "If ye're lucky there's a blanket that hasn't been chewed by mice. But don't expect a mint on the pillow."

"Good to know expectations are low."

"Aye. Keeps disappointment from knockin' ye flat."

Her words are sharp, but the way her voice dips at the end tells me she's not talking about cabins anymore. And I wonder what else this land has taken from her besides a stepfather and a crumbling fence line.

I fall in step behind her, boots crunching gravel, the Texas dusk pressing down warm and heavy. I'm no longer thinking about the road behind me or the endless drive back to New York. I'm thinking about this place, this woman, and a cow with opinions who might just change everything.

And somehow, in spite of the chaos—or maybe because of it—I know one thing for sure.

I'm not going anywhere just yet.

For more Patrick and Mharie click here: A Highland Homestead Christmas

Also by

The Wild Child Reckless Series

This is Growing Up

She was his best friend's little sister and completely off-limits—until one unforgettable night changed everything. Now Delilah is famous, engaged, and untouchable... but Alexander isn't giving up that easily. Because he had her once, and he's not letting her go again.

This is Meant to Be

She's promised to another. He's risking everything to keep her. Lillian was never supposed to fall for Jensen—but now that she has, neither of them is willing to let go, no matter how high the price.

This is Taking Chances

He shattered her heart once. Now he's back—not just to make amends, but to prove he's worthy of the family he never knew he had. A deaf drummer with a broken past. A single mother who swore she'd never look back. One love story that refuses to stay buried.

This is Starting Over**

She was the one girl he swore off limits. Now she's all grown up, in danger—and back under his protection.

This time, he's not sure he can walk away.

Foster, Inc. Novellas
Jack Frost, CEO

She's his assistant. He's her father's enemy. Pretending to be engaged might save his business deal, but when sparks turn into something real, Jack has to decide if falling for Maisie is worth the risk—or the scandal.

Willow Glen Series
From Feud to Forever*

She stole the land he spent twenty years trying to reclaim. He's determined to make her regret it—until their bickering turns into banter and the sparks start flying. In a small town full of gossip and grudge matches, Adam and Christiane are about to find out that the line between hate and love is thinner than a fence post.

A Highland Homestead Christmas**

Also part of the Piper Falls Christmas Collection

She came to Texas to settle her stepfather's estate. He only meant to stop by for a cow. By one fake engagement, a meddling town, and a feud-hungry uncle later, Mharie Campbell and Patrick Williams are knee-deep in Christmas chaos—and each other. In Piper Falls, where traditions fun deep and every secret sparks a rumor, they'll have to decide if what started as pretend is worth keeping for real.

Sons of Santoro Series

Tasting Sin-

Also part of the Sexy as Sin: Las Vegas World

She's the boss with everything to lose. He's the chef with nothing left to prove.

When a high-stakes sabotage threatens Sienna Moreau's Las Vegas hotel, she turns to the one man who infuriates and tempts her in equal measure—Luca Santoro. In a city built on secrets, desire becomes their sharpest weapon... but trusting each other might be the biggest gamble of all.

Monroe Strategic Capital Series

The Christmas Waffle*

He's a grumpy CEO with a plan for everything. She's the too-young, off-limits assistant who blows it all to hell with one unforgettable night—and one life-changing surprise. Now, with secrets, misunderstandings, and a baby on the line, they'll have to decide if their second chance is worth risking everything for.

*2025 $0.99 Preorder

** 2026 $0.99 Preorder

From the Author

Thank you for reading!!! If you have a moment please leave a review- they are so incredibly important to indie authors. I always loved reading, and now I have a separate love of writing. I hope you stick around and join me in this amazing adventure! I am always looking to connect! You can find me in the following places.

SmutTok Made Me Do It Facebook Group

Juliet McKinleys Book Nook

Sign Up for my newsletter here so that you never miss a beat, giveaway or sneak peek-

Newsletter   julietmckinley.myflodesk.com

TikTok   @JulieyMcKinleyAuthor

Instagram   @JulietMckinleyAuthor

Facebook   Juliet McKinley